War on th

WAR ON THE MARGINS

Libby Cone

DUCKWORTH OVERLOOK
London and New York

First paperback edition 2010
First published in 2009 by
Duckworth Overlook
90-93 Cowcross Street
London, EC1M 6BF
Tel: 020 7490 7300
Fax: 020 7490 0080
info@duckworth-publishers.co.uk
www.ducknet.co.uk

The right of Libby Cone to be identified as the Author of
the Work has been asserted by her in accordance with
the Copyright, Designs and Patents Act 1988.

A catalogue record for this book is available
from the British Library

ISBN 978 0 7156 3972 6

With the exception of the note on page 212, all documents
and letters in this book are real and directly quoted or,
when not in English, translated as closely as possible.
Any abbreviations or irregularities in spelling and
punctuation were present in the original.

Typeset by Ray Davies
Printed in Great Britain by
J F Print Ltd, Sparkford, Somerset

CHAPTER 1

St Helier, Jersey, Channel Islands

Marlene Zimmer dropped into the chair in her sitting room with the paper, knowing what it would say before she opened it.

The Evening Post

21 October 1940

First Order relating to measures against Jews: Concerning the Registration of Jews in Jersey

In pursuance of an Order of the Chief of the German Military Administration in France (registered by Act of the Royal Court, dated October 21st, 1940), and in virtue of the power delegated to me by the Bailiff, all Jews must present themselves for registration at the Aliens Office, No. 6 Hill Street, St. Helier, on Wednesday and Thursday, October 23rd and 24th, 1940, between the hours of 10 a.m. and 4 p.m. For the purposes of this Order, persons are deemed to be Jews who belong or have belonged to the Jewish religion or who have more than two Jewish grandparents.

  Grandparents who belong or have belonged to the Jewish religion are deemed to be Jews.

  The particulars to be provided upon registration are:

1. Surname.
2. Christian name. [sic]
3. Date of birth.
4. Place of birth.
5. Sex.
6. Family status.
7. Profession.

```
  8.Religious faith.
  9.Length of uninterrupted residence in the
Island.


The declaration of the head of the family will
suffice for the whole family.

CLIFFORD ORANGE
Chief Aliens Officer
```

Another notice followed, from C. W. Duret Aubin, the Attorney General, 'concerning the marking of Jewish business undertaking with signs saying "*JUEDISCHES GESCHAEFT*", "Jewish Undertaking"'.

Her hands trembled, rattling the paper. She got up, made some weak tea. That day the Order had been revealed to the personnel in the Aliens Office, where Marlene was employed as a clerk.

Last spring, even people like Marlene, who didn't listen to the news very much, started tuning in to the BBC to hear about the Nazi fist rapidly closing around Europe. When France fell and the troops were evacuated from Dunkirk, the Islanders, British but with many French cultural ties, finally had the war brought home to their little feudal paradise of beaches and farms. Their fears were reflected in the faces of wounded Dunkirk troops brought over from St Malo. People sat up at night, talking about what would happen next in their lives, affected now by more than a dent in the tourist traffic. The Jersey States Government officials were ferrying back and forth between St Helier and London, returning daily with ever grimmer facial expressions. People began to talk about invasion, and Marlene lost her appetite. On 10 June, Italy declared war upon Britain, and the Aliens Office girls had to busy themselves with the reclassification of Italians, who were promptly locked up along with the Germans at the internment centre at Grouville, as enemies. This extra work was off-putting. Pauline, a tall girl who resembled an auburn-haired Vivien Leigh, complained as she walked to the cinema with Marlene and the other girls, 'Why were they friends, and now enemies? They are the same people. It makes no sense!'

'It's just reclassification,' someone said.

'But didn't they get sent to Grouville?'

'They might be dangerous – who knows?'

Marlene did not wish to trouble herself with such thoughts. She allowed the other girls to argue with Pauline, who seemed awfully concerned about the Italians. Marlene was plain. She had, perhaps, Vivien Leigh's eyebrows, but not her exquisite bone structure. She had Gracie Fields' wispy hair, but not her dazzling smile. Marlene lived in the flat off Queens Road where she had been born a little over twenty-five years before, a fact she did not like to dwell upon, as she was still unmarried. She had her family photographs, her late mother's kitchen things, her late father's silver goblet, the old wireless, and a few pieces of comfortable furniture. A bit too impervious to the growing unease around her, she assumed that the War would spare Jersey, would just be reports on the wireless as she went about her life, a life that, if examined more closely, might be called 'aimless'.

On the 19th, Jurat Dorey had returned from London and announced that Jersey and the other Channel Islands, Guernsey, Alderney and Sark, so close to fallen France, had been deemed indefensible and were to be declared a 'demilitarised zone'. The Germans would be allowed to take over! Chaos followed; thousands of people were haphazardly evacuated, leaving behind their homes, cars and farms. Thousands of dogs and cats were put down by the departing families, filling the harbourside streets with mute, flushed children who could not cry any more, and dazed adults torn from their pets as a last cruelty before being torn from their homes. Abandoned cows roamed the streets. People unable to leave on the last ship returned to find their homes looted. The girls talked of nothing else all day, and Marlene spent many of her evenings listening to the wireless and weeping.

In late June, just when things were seemingly quieter, German planes appeared before dusk and bore down on the port, and the one in Guernsey, bombing and strafing. They had not been informed of the demilitarisation, and the blood of farmers mixed with the pulp of the tomatoes they had hoped to load onto the boats. Burning warehouses lit up the night sky. Those who had decided to stay behind lay sleepless in their beds, berating themselves or their nearest relative, or looked into their mirrors and wondered if the face that looked back at them was destined to waste away from starvation or bear the mark of the lash. They woke to a sky the colour of filthy rags. Two days later, as they were burying their dead, the message went out that everyone was to fly white flags of surrender. All privately-owned guns were confiscated. People emptied the shops in anticipation. Troop transport planes roared into the commandeered airports, and the Islands were suddenly inundated with German soldiers and the Nazi civilians who were to administer the occupation.

Instantly the Italians and Germans interned at Grouville were no longer enemies, but friends. They were released, and Marlene and the staff followed Mr Orange's orders to reclassify them accordingly.

Churchill had been convinced of the Islands' lack of strategic importance. Hitler saw them as a staging area for the attack on

England, which Goering thought would last two or three weeks. Then they would be the gateway to Europe. Everywhere the Germans communicated the message *We Own You*. A flag bearing a swastika rose over Fort Regent; Marlene had seen a few in newsreels, always used to illustrate some monstrous violent act or other. She took to avoiding the streets that offered a view of the Fort and the ugly flag, but you couldn't avoid the Germans everywhere, with their air of superiority and barely suppressed violence. The soldiers seemed to make an effort to be friendly, but they bought up what was left of the fruit and vegetables with the strange *Reichsmarks* everyone now had to use, and presided over the sending of large quantities of produce and other supplies to Occupied France. Rations were made more stringent to allow for this.

Strange, solitary men lurked on the street corners, not even trying to be inconspicuous, paying close attention to every conversation between citizens. *We Own You*. Some said they were secret police, and if they caught you saying anything they didn't like they would arrest you. The strict rationing of petrol and the commandeering of cars, which were ferried over to France, led to a run on the bicycle shops and the reappearance of horse-drawn wagons and carts.

Planes were always roaring in the sky, going to France, or, more ominously, to England. After 15 July islanders were allowed to listen to the BBC again, and thousands of trembling hands turned on the wireless to hear the reports of the Battle of Britain raging almost overhead. Marlene listened and despaired, even though it seemed Britain was holding up its side. The Nazis' consternation over the unexpected British defence was reflected in the Germans' behaviour; recently a soldier had stabbed a civilian at the Alexandra Hotel. A series of warnings against rowdyism and careless driving carried more

11

weight than usual, since the Nazi solution to everything was violence. *We Own You*.

Late August brought warm, dry weather and nightly firefights and bombing, either targeting the airport, striking houses adjacent, or on the nearby French coast. In September they entered the libraries and piled up the books they did not like – anything that was by a Jewish author or described something of Jewish interest. They set fire to them, and the smoke polluted the air like hatred. *We Own You*. Fear was a staple; hunger threatened. Life was turned upside down and one learned to scurry down the street without saying much to anyone, to avoid the gaze of the soldiers, some of whom easily took offence.

At the Aliens Office, the other employees were put off by the extra paperwork involved in this Jewish-registration business. Mr Orange, almost eager to carry out the German Order, had been at his most officious that morning. Tall and slightly stooped, with wrinkled face and light, bushy eyebrows, he fancied himself to be avuncular, though nobody else did. Since the Occupation, he had expressed his new-found feeling of importance unreservedly. Orders from the *Feldkommandantur* to Bailiff Coutanche regarding the many segments of the large foreign-born population all came to his desk. This new Order was somewhat unusual; he had gathered the girls into his office to explain it to them. Music tinkled softly on the wireless; later on in the day they would hear snatches of Lord Haw-Haw pontificating on German Overseas Radio.

'Ladies,' Mr Orange began, clearing his throat. 'I trust you understand this Order?' He looked at them over his horn-rimmed glasses.

'Yes, sir,' they said, uncertainly.

'It is up to this office to carry out the Orders to the letter, so that Bailiff Coutanche and our, er, German guests are satisfied. All Jews will be coming in to register, and I ask that you be as helpful as possible in this endeavour.'

'Mr Orange, isn't this only for aliens?'

Pauline looked quizzically at Mr Orange.

'No, Pauline. This is for ALL the Jews.'

Pauline said nothing.

Marlene's chest felt tight. Why did Jersey Jews have to register in the Aliens Office? Were they suddenly not British subjects? She took a deep breath and tried to relax. I don't count, she thought. I only have two Jewish grandparents.

'We just need to do what they want, and they'll leave us be,' he had said, looking optimistic, but avoiding their gaze.

Who is 'us', Marlene thought.

What am I, Marlene thought.

She stopped thinking for the rest of the working day, and went on filing, typing, sorting. Her head felt hollowed out; the thoughts she was emptying it of were so enormous that there was nothing left to think about. She forced herself to keep making small talk with the other girls. No, she didn't want to go to the cinema that night to see a German film; she was busy that evening, but later in the week would be splendid.

The thoughts kept returning. Am *I* one? Do I have to register? What will happen? Her late father had been Jewish; he had died when she was a young child, but her mother had told her, and shown her the wine goblet he had left for her, calling it a 'kiddish', or something. She certainly couldn't call herself much of a Christian; she had stopped going to church very young, and her mother had never made a fuss over it, not going much herself. They went to her father's grave in the Jewish section of the Almorah cemetery every six months or

13

so, each putting a little pebble on his headstone as they saw other Jews doing at their own loved ones' graves. Now her mother was buried near her father, just outside the Jewish section.

Marlene jumped up and checked the clock. It was half-past six, well before the eleven p.m. curfew. She wanted to visit the graves, but it was dark outside. Even though she could bicycle there in the dark, it might arouse suspicion. She paced back and forth. Then she pulled an old overcoat out of the closet. She bustled around the flat, picking up a few handkerchiefs, a toothbrush, some underwear, a small bar of soap, a tiny sewing kit, money. She stuffed these things in the pockets and hung the coat on the back of her bedroom door. She sat down again, picked up the paper, and tried to do the crossword puzzle. It was impossible to concentrate. She got up, rummaged through drawers, and found her father's goblet. She held it reverently and looked at the indecipherable Hebrew writing on it. She barely remembered her father except from photographs, but did recall his hugging her and their throwing a big red rubber ball. Her mother had adored her father, always had pleasant recollections of him, and never remarried after his death. What if he were alive today? What would happen to him? He would certainly have to register. Nobody knew exactly what the jerries were up to with the Jews, but nobody had heard anything good. There was no love lost between the Jews and certain non-Jewish islanders, and some people talked.

After a small supper she switched on the wireless; the war had made her a regular listener. Churchill was going on in his jowly voice, addressing the French as well as the English. 'Here in London, which *Herr* Hitler said he will reduce to ashes, and whose aeroplanes are now bombarding' – (Marlene

14

shut her eyes) – 'our people are bearing up.' He launched into a summary of the state of affairs. 'We have command of the sea. They wish to carve up our Empire as if it were a fowl … Have hope and faith, for all will come right,' he said, after a long description of the indignities already visited upon France, and the future obliteration of French culture desired by Hitler. 'I will not go into detail; hostile ears are listening' made Marlene shiver. She kept reassuring herself that she had only two Jewish grandparents, so she didn't really count.

CHAPTER 2

St Helier, Jersey, Channel Islands

22 October 1940

Marlene was up early after a largely sleepless night. She choked down some breakfast, got on her bicycle, and rode to the office. A queue of people stood waiting in the cold sunlight. She recognised Mr Davidson, who ran a small grocery shop where she occasionally bought tea. She smiled at him as she approached the back entrance; he smiled back nervously. They all came in over the next two days: Miss Bercu, Mrs Blampied, Mr Davidson, Mr Emmanuel, Mr Finkelstein, Mr Goldman, Mrs Hurban, Mr Jacobs, Mrs Lloyd, old Mrs Marks, Mr Simon, Mrs Still and Miss Viner. They were a little nervous, some of them, but resigned to comply with the latest indignity of the Occupation. The girls helped them fill out cards, and gave signs to the Jewish business owners. It was strange, since some of these people had never thought of themselves as Jewish. Indeed, some knew the clerks from church.

Marlene was helping Mr Davidson. He instructed her to list him as a 'Christian'. She remembered seeing him sitting with his wife in a back pew when she used to go to church. She stopped Mr Orange.

'Sir,' she said. 'Is he supposed to register? His paternal grandfather was a Jew, but he does not know about his maternal grandparents.'

Mr Orange looked at Mr Davidson, who sat quietly in an office chair. 'Is that right, Mr Davidson?'

'Yes, sir. My mother's parents died when I was little. I'm Church of England, though, sir. Doesn't that disqualify me?'

'Well, Mr Davidson, you came in to register, did you not?'

Yes; he came in to register. He was an obedient Jersey citizen.

'Fill the card in, please, Marlene. Actually,' he said, hesitating for a moment, 'let's have it here a minute.' She handed it over. Taking out his fountain pen, Mr Orange scribbled a note in the margin, then handed it back to Marlene. 'Good day to you, Mr Davidson.'

Mr Davidson said nothing. Marlene looked at the note:

Mr Davidson has stated that he has always belonged to the Christian community; so far as he is aware, his father did also. Believes that one of his grandparents was a Jew, but knows nothing about the others. – C.O.

Marlene marvelled at her hands the rest of the day. They filled out and carried cards, typed memoranda, made tea. They did all the things they were used to doing while her mind was elsewhere. She kept adding up her grandparents. Two Jewish, two not. Wasn't that all right? Why did Mr Davidson, and, she later learned, others with two Jewish grandparents, have to register? Why did *anyone* have to? Weren't they all stuck on the Islands for the duration? How long would this 'duration' be? She glanced at her fellow clerks, who had again become lackadaisical as the Germans settled in, filling out forms, stamping passports, performing all the minutiae of office work without thinking. They would finish at four, have supper, and then go to the cinema, perhaps to see *The Jew Suss*. They weren't nervous like Marlene. Why was she so nervous all the time? Her mother would chide her for her bitten nails, her toe-

17

tapping, her frequent sighs. Her nerves were most likely to blame for her being unmarried in her mid-twenties; it certainly wasn't her mother's fault. Marlene the fretful, Marlene the worrywart, Marlene the fussy old maid. Valerian was no help. Drinking gave her a headache. She simply had to put up with her nerves as part and parcel of herself. At least everyone was used to them, so they would not seem noteworthy now.

After work she pedalled to Almorah cemetery in the fading light and visited her mother's grave. She laid a few late autumn flowers upon it and stood back, gazing at the stone. She had forgotten prayer. She stood and remembered her mother. Her mum had been a regular sort with a frequent smile but slight sadness in her eyes if you looked at her closely. She had bustled about her work at Boots and in their kitchen at home, had made most of Marlene's clothing and taught her to bake biscuits. She frequently talked about Marlene's late father, and was clearly proud to have had such a kind and unusual husband who let her keep her wages (she spent them on the household anyway), helped with the washing up and shopping, and was attentive to Marlene, even after a long day working for Mr Dumosch the potato merchant. Although Marlene's mother had attended the occasional dance after his early death, she had never again indulged in courtship, happy to raise alone the daughter born of her ten-year marriage with Ted.

Marlene then walked the bike the few steps to her father's grave, stooped to pick up a pebble, and laid it on the top of his stone. She performed again for him the same prayerless standing devotion. Then her nervousness rose to the surface: she was alone, she had two Jewish grandparents, the shops were running out of rationed food, the bloody jerries were everywhere, it was getting cold. She sank to her knees in tears; she stared helplessly at her father's headstone and sobbed into her hands. It was growing darker. She was afraid to stay longer, afraid to go home, afraid to do anything. Well, that wouldn't get her anywhere, would it? She took a deep breath, hauled herself up from the gravel, and walked her bicycle back to the front gate. As she passed the caretaker's building, she heard voices from around the corner: a woman's laughter, a man's chuckle. She tried to see them out of the corner of her eye as she passed; she couldn't, but she recognised Pauline's unmistakable giggle and the man's distinctive German accent. 'So,' she thought, 'Pauline's a bloody jerrybag.' She hardened her facial expression, though nobody could see it. Had Pauline recognised her? Was the German there as a spy, to find out Jews? She shouldn't have placed the pebble! It was too late now. She quickened her pedalling, arriving home breathless.

CHAPTER 3

St Helier, Jersey

22 October 1940

Marlene parked her bicycle in front of the flat and went in. She sat on the couch and covered her face with her hands. What was she going to do? Pauline and the German had seen her; that was evidence enough that she had had a Jewish relative. She would have to register. It was probably fine; she was just nervous.

She took the overcoat off the bedroom door, got her sewing box, and turned on the wireless. She was astonished to hear mention of the Channel Islands, with evacuated children giving their greetings from England, and a few people speaking Jersey French. Her heart pounded with excitement, but she continued her task. With a seam ripper, she separated the lining in the right side from the outer material, deciding that sitting would be too uncomfortable if she sewed things into the back. She walked around the flat, looking at all her belongings. She had some tea left from last week's ration. Taking an envelope from her desk, she emptied the tea into it, sealed it, and placed it in the overcoat compartment, sewing through the envelope with two stitches to anchor it to the lining. She couldn't put much more money in because there was a limit to what you could withdraw from the bank, even after the evacuation. Opening her jewellery box, she removed her mother's pearls and sewed them into the lining. If she took all the things out of the right pocket and put them into the left, it didn't look too unbalanced. She decided to sew some underwear in, followed it with a few handkerchiefs and some soap, an envelope of matches and a photo of her father in a little cloth bag, and sewed the lining back inside the right side of the coat. She replaced it on the door, ate her last piece of bread and butter, and went to sleep.

The next morning she reported to work. Pauline paid no attention to her. Mr Orange was out of the office for the morning. When he returned in the afternoon, he looked at letters that had come in from Island attorneys eager to report the Jewish ancestry of their clients and asking what to do about registering their businesses. He looked at other letters and then called Marlene into his office.

'Marlene,' he began, not looking straight at her, 'uh, is, ah, "Zimmer" a Jewish name?'

'Yes, sir, it is. My father was Jewish. But my mother was not, and I am not.'

'Right. Well, perhaps to be thorough, hadn't you better register?' He handed her the form.

'Mr Orange, won't you put a note on it as you did for Mr Davidson? He only had one or two Jewish grandparents, too.'

'Yes, of course.'

Her hands shook so, it looked like another person's handwriting. She dropped the form on Mr Orange's desk, ran out to the WC, and was sick. At least it stopped her hands shaking. She washed her face without looking in the mirror and returned to work. Nobody paid her any mind, least of all Pauline, who had most likely turned her in. It was best not to attract attention, anyway. When they asked her if she wanted to go to the cinema that night, she accepted.

The film was *Sieg im Westen*. Someone said it meant 'Victory in the West'. As Marlene read the subtitles, she understood that it was about the fall of Holland, Belgium and France. Why anyone would want to watch such rubbish was beyond her. It was full of tanks and aeroplanes, people killing each other. She was sitting well into the row in the civilians' section. Some of the office girls were trying to sit on the outside so they could flirt with the German soldiers across the aisle. Marlene tried not to watch. She tried to think of what else she could sew into the overcoat, but that made her too frantic, and it wouldn't do to cry in the cinema, not when the enemy was watching. She tried looking at the head of someone a few rows ahead; that didn't do. She tried following the violins in the soundtrack. That distracted her for a while. Her stomach growled with hunger. Suddenly, a small item was passed to her. A tiny chocolate bar! It must be from one of the Germans; it was too dark to read the printing on it, but she was sure it was German, provided by one of the fellows keeping company with one of her colleagues, no doubt. As she watched the three countries beaten to a pulp by the German forces, she let the small piece of chocolate melt on her tongue. She eventually closed her eyes so she could concentrate on the taste instead of the carnage. She thought of her father. He must have given her chocolate when she was little. She had to remember that; he hadn't just given her her name, a name that was getting her into hot water with the jerries.

CHAPTER 4

St Helier, Jersey

October 1940

Marlene decided to go to Mr Davidson's shop for her tea ration. She pedalled over on Saturday afternoon. She could not get used to the big 'Jewish Undertaking' signs she saw every so often. It made her think of undertakers. Mr Davidson, of course, had one on the door of his establishment.

'Hello, dear,' he said. God, he looked awful. All thin and shaky.

'Good afternoon, Mr Davidson. How are you?'

'How am I? I'm bloody terrible, that's how I am! Why are they after me, Marlene? What did I do, that they have to put their bloody sign on my door? I'm Church of England, I am! A whole lot of good the Church is doing me now! I think the Church is spying on me at night. I see the bloody vicar in disguise, walking around outside my house. He knows where I keep my money!'

His speech was fast, agitated. It was a little strange. Marlene was uncomfortable.

'Um, I, uh, just came in for some tea.' She handed him her ration slip.

'Oh,' he said, suddenly, with no emotion. 'I only have Earl Grey left. Will that do?'

'Yes, that's fine.' It really wasn't; she didn't care for Earl Grey, but she wanted to leave and she did not want to seem rude by not buying anything.

'Well, then. Anything else?'

'No, thank you, Mr Davidson. Good day.'

'Be careful, Marlene. Don't let the bloody Church people find you!' His agitation returned again. Like turning up the wireless.

She ducked out of the shop with her tea and jumped onto her bicycle. He was acting very oddly indeed. Back at home, she poured the tea leaves into the caddy. Then she sewed her father's cup into the left side of her coat.

CHAPTER 5

18 November 1940

The Evening Post

Royal Courts of Jersey
Defence Regulation No 174
The Second Order relating to Measures against the
Jews

All Jewish economic undertakings, all Jews, all
husbands and wives of Jews, and all bodies
corporate which are not economic undertakings but
more than one third of whose members or managers
are Jews shall ... declare to the Bailiff ... the
shares belonging ... to them, their beneficial
interest in the business, their sleeping interest
in economic undertakings and loans to such
undertakings, their real estate and interest
therein.

   'NOTE: ... [under] the power vested ... by the
Bailiff ... that undertakings, persons and bodies
specified in ... the said Order must send or
deliver the required declarations to the Aliens
Office (signed "Clifford Orange.")'

===

Jersey 23/11/40
Chief Aliens Officer
Hill Street
St. Helier

Sir,

With reference to order relating to measures
against Jews dated 18/11/40 I am not sure whether
I come under the province of the above order, but

in case I do, I declare the following: I am
running a small grocery shop which I am winding
up at present and beyond a small banking account
I have no other assets or property whatever.

Yours truly,
Nathan Davidson

===

11th January, 1941

Mr N. Davidson
35, Stopford Road
St. Helier

Sir,

I refer to our recent interview regarding the
Orders received from Field Command 515 regarding
your business, and now have to inform you, as you
have elected to close down rather than have an
Aryan administrator appointed, that the authority
requires your business to be wound up before
January 25th, 1941.
    I have to require you, therefore, to proceed to
make your arrangements accordingly, and to inform
me in writing when the winding up of your
business is actually completed.

Yours faithfully,
Charles Duret Aubin
Attorney General

===

Attorney General's Chambers
Jersey

January 23rd, 1941

Sir,

In accordance to your instructions I beg to
inform you that I have finished the winding up of
my Business at 35 Stopford Road today, January
23rd 1941, the blind on the window pulled down
and a notice 'CLOSED' displayed.

Yours truly,
N. Davidson

CHAPTER 6

St Helier, Jersey

March 1941

The winter had passed. Mrs Marks had died. Everyone was getting thinner; milk and butter were usually only available on the black market. It was more lucrative for the farmers and shopkeepers to sell to the Germans than to their fellow islanders. Some people stole things back from the Germans. There was a brisk traffic of goods from Occupied France to the Islands. Islanders who were caught stealing or selling on the black market took the return route from the Islands to France, destined for prison at Caen or Lille. They didn't mind; they received Red Cross parcels in prison, and were able to regain a little weight.

Islanders had heard Churchill in February, reporting on how well the English had held up under the winter's bombing, on the low rates of crime and illness in England over the past months, how they had beaten back the 'Italian invaders of Egypt'. Not a word about the occupied Islands, though everyone yearned not to be forgotten. Which was worse: to flee into Underground tunnels most nights and sit in the damp as the bombs thudded down, or to see one's street overrun with German soldiers and vehicles, and the sunny beaches pockmarked with mines? To have to watch one's step, hold one's tongue, keep a pleasant face so as not to upset the wrong person and end up in prison? To find you couldn't trust your local government?

Mr Davidson had been forced to close his shop; it was a

'Jewish undertaking'. Other shops were being sold off; Mr Orange was pleased at how smoothly it was going. Marlene wanted to spit at him. It had long ago dawned on her that she was not being silly at all, that this was indeed a very serious matter, and that her instincts were correct.

One morning, Mr Orange gathered the girls in his office. His tan jacket looked a bit ragged, but he had a crisp handkerchief in the pocket. He cleared his throat, looked over his glasses, and gave them some instructions on the classification of British-born and Island-born citizens. Next, he announced the latest order from the *Feldkommandantur*.

'We have a new order, ladies. We need to reclassify all Jews as foreigners.' He took up a blank file card. 'Every Jew will have his or her card marked with a red stripe like so.' He drew a thick red line diagonally across the card with a pen filled with red ink. 'Then we put a large "J" in the lower left corner like so.' As he wrote the 'J', he went over and over it in red ink. 'Try not to obscure the photo or any writing. Pauline, why don't you do this, while I instruct the other girls in another little duty?'

Pauline did not look eager to commence, but she stood up and went into the filing area. Marlene sat dumbstruck as Mr Orange went on about inaccurate typing and the need to file Irish citizens properly. She eventually left with the others. She walked by Pauline as a phone on the desk rang. As Pauline ran to pick it up, Marlene, her mouth dry as cotton, said, 'I'll finish these for you.'

Pauline gave her a grateful nod as she took up the receiver. Quickly Marlene looked at the two cards Pauline had left to file. Viner and Zimmer. The rest of the alphabet was doomed. She made a quick show of rummaging through the card file and scribbling with pens while surreptitiously folding the cards lengthwise and slipping them into the sleeve of her blouse. She smiled and nodded at Pauline, who was still on the telephone. Taking her handbag with her into the WC, she ripped the cards to shreds and dropped the pieces into it. She and Miss Viner had officially ceased to exist.

CHAPTER 7

Carefully spacing the columns, Mr Orange's secretary dutifully compiled the list, along with many other lists that he had to sign. He distractedly scribbled his signature and went on to his other duties, most of which would ruin the lives of others.

```
17th March, 1941

The Bailiff of Jersey

Re. Registration of Jews.

Sir,

I have the honour to refer to your Memorandum (W
30/17) regarding the Registration of Jews and to
report that the filing cards of Registered Jews
have been marked and fixed with a red cross strip
and included in the Registration Files for
foreigners, as directed.
  A list (in triplicate) of Jews registered in
Jersey, showing the nationality of each person,
is forwarded to you herewith.

I have the honour to be, Sir,
Your obedient servant,

Clifford Orange
Chief Aliens Officer


===================================================
```

List of Jews registered in Jersey, showing
nationality of each person.

SURNAME	CHRISTIAN [sic] NAMES	NATIONALITY
BERCU	Hedy	Roumanian
BLAMPIED née VANABBE	Marianne	British (by marriage) (Dutch by birth)
DAVIDSON	Nathan	Egyptian (by naturalisation) (Roumanian by birth)
EMMANUEL	Victor	British (by naturalisation) (German by birth)
FINKELSTEIN	John Max	Roumanian
GOLDMAN	Hyam	British
HURBAN née BLOD	Margaret	German (formerly Austrian)
JACOBS	John	British
LLOYD née SILVER	Esther Pauline	British
SIMON	Samuel Selig	British
STILL née MARKS	Ruby Ellen	British

CHAPTER 8

Jersey

March 1941

She didn't go back to her flat. At the end of the working day,
she put her coat on, got onto her bicycle, and began pedalling
frantically. It was only an hour till dark, and she had no idea
where to go.

She found herself heading west; the streets were almost
bare of pedestrians and cyclists, so she could pedal quietly
along without raising too much attention. She took the shore
road deliberately because the sharp ocean breeze would deter
passers-by. A few jerries in trucks were on the road; inhaling
great draughts of salty air, she tried not to look at them. They
certainly paid her no mind.

Soon she was in the parish of St Brelade, a seaside paradise.
It was almost dark. She dismounted her bicycle and pushed it,
gripping the handles tightly as she wondered what to do next.
She wanted to sit down and think; would she ever be able to?
Would sitting with a cup of tea be something she would ever
be able to do again? Would she ever 'sit' again, or would she
lean, huddle, crouch, or cower? She saw the sign for the St
Brelade's Bay Hotel and walked towards it. It was a beautiful
building with official-looking vehicles parked outside. A few
jerries stood around the entrance, smoking and talking. When
they looked at her, she managed a tiny smile and walked by.
It seemed to have been taken over by the soldiers for a barracks. Should she try to work there as a maid? She was not
listed as a Jew any more. What if Pauline's boyfriend lived

there? The idea was too frightening. She walked her bicycle further along the road. She was shaking now; she was filled with panic and needed to get off the street. The St Brelade cemetery was up ahead on a hill above the ocean. She had a sense of *déjà vu*; wasn't it just a few months ago that Pauline and her German beau had spotted her at the Jewish section of the cemetery in St Helier? There was no time to make a fuss; she had to hide.

She walked with agonising slowness to the cemetery gate and approached the small chapel next to the church. She pulled her bicycle out of sight of the road and stood with her back to the chapel, facing the cold ocean. The cemetery was deserted. She turned and looked at the door of the chapel. There was a hasp, but no lock. She took deep breaths, looked around. There was a jerry guard tower on a cliff to the right; had they seen her? Their light was not yet lit. She quickly opened the door and slipped inside. When she was able to calm the pounding of her heart she reached out and pulled her bicycle in just before the tower light went on. That and the tiny bit of light from sunset coming through the window outlined shelves on the far wall, with various candles and devotional cards. Keeping her head below the level of the window, she pulled out some of the kneeling cushions and arranged a kind of bed. Well, here she was, crouching. She removed her coat. It would be important to keep it clean so as not to attract attention. She did not want to rip the lining until necessary. A few biscuits secreted in her pockets were her supper. She carefully rolled her coat into a ball, rested her head on it, and lay awake for hours in the cold, damp air.

CHAPTER 9

La Rocquaise, St Brelade, Jersey

March 1941

The swede is not a glamorous vegetable. Hard, unlovely, humble. Something to use as a side dish at the occasional meal, hot and mashed and dressed with butter – maybe a tiny sprinkle of nutmeg. Now it was a vegetable of exigency, the main course, the roast, the joint, the centrepiece, the star.

Suzanne Malherbe was in charge of the menu at *La Rocquaise*, as well as the director of graphic design. To her the swede had become just another medium, a *tabula rasa*. When there was enough wood to be had, she would just boil them up on the stove, *chou-navettes*, topped with a pinhead-sized lump of butter and a grind of pepper, and hungrily devour them with Lucille. Now that fuel supplies were unreliable, she had to be more creative. She found that slightly dried-out swedes were more amenable to being formed into sculptures and bas-reliefs; they had a somewhat more yielding consistency to the paring knife. She kept a small collection of them undergoing this curing process in a box in the cellar. Today she had two good-sized ones; she peeled them and put them on the cutting board. The peels would be dried for soup.

Suzanne stood back and regarded them gravely. Taking up her knife, she began cutting regular slices and putting them in a single layer on another board. Then she took each slice and made it something; one was a flower with an eye in the centre. Another was a rabbit with wings. She carefully formed a breast with a clock, a seashell with wheels, a pair of pursed lips. She arranged the slices on two plates, poured two glasses of white wine, put it all on a tray, and took it out to Lucille in the dining room. Lucille rose, smiled and kissed her, then looked intently at the plates.

'*Cherie*! They're wonderful! You are a true genius! Without a doubt, nobody eats their swedes this way in Nantes.'

'Thank you, *cherie*.'

'To the Resistance!' they cried, clinking glasses. They took up their forks and slowly chewed the transformed swedes. A half loaf of potato bread on the table, initially shunned, was more palatable after their first glass of wine.

'It is at two?' asked Suzanne.

'Yes. I already have the songs typed.'

'Wonderful! And the disguises?'

'Let's wear the same wigs and different coats this time.'

'Lovely!'

Suzanne cleared the dishes away and began to brew some tea. 'We need to celebrate before our revolutionary action.'

'But of course!'

Lucille took out a flat box containing a profusion of pastel-coloured tissue paper. Another box contained pens and coloured pencils. All were laid on the dining table. Lucille removed a large envelope from underneath the blank papers and took out about twenty variously handwritten and type-written notes. 'Please proofread them once more, *cherie*. I worry I may not have copied your German correctly.'

Suzanne scanned the pages. They were copies of a song the women had written.

> We are the heroes of the Master Race,
> We are the German soldiers.

We have defeated all of Europe
And seen the coast of Dover.

And if I come home for the holidays,
And my wife's belly is big as a boulder,
'Baby, don't get mad at me,' she'll say,
'The Fatherland needs more soldiers!'

And if I come home for the holidays…

My skin was burnt to blisters,
As I warmed up in Africa's weather,
The meat was rotten, the water stank,
My burnt eyes as thick as leather.

And if I come home for the holidays …

And round and round the world this dance of death
Goes faster and faster,
Until we can no longer fight;
And overthrow our masters!

And if I come home for the holidays
My wife will be looking much older,
'Baby, to bed!' she'll say to me
'The Fatherland needs more soldiers!'

'I wish we could write music to it; they would be singing it all over the island. I will add some finishing touches.' Suzanne took up a pen and made a few corrections. After she had blotted the ink and pronounced herself satisfied, the two women began balling up the papers like so much rubbish. They stuffed all the wads into two large handbags. Then they repaired upstairs to dress. Lucille took out a brown wig and stuffed her short red hair under it. Suzanne was handed a blonde wig; she did the same. Lucille, so used to dressing in various costumes in her younger days of gender exploration and self-portraiture, took easily to most disguises, although she preferred male dress. Suzanne, who had used the androgynous name Marcel Moore on her work as a graphic designer, had never thought of herself as a costume artist who played with identities; she was learning quickly. She removed her smock and trousers and pulled on a thick sweater and a black wool skirt. Lucille added some *bourgeois* costume jewellery to her wine-coloured dress. They threw on shapeless lightweight coats. A little touch of lipstick and they were off.

First they walked past the St Brelade's Bay Hotel. They bought newspapers, which they tucked under their arms; these could be used as tubes for launching the crumpled paper through a half-open car window. There were few cars there now, so they proceeded to the cemetery where the graveside service had begun.

A young enlisted man had committed suicide. It probably had something to do with the deployment of the *Afrika Korps*. This occasion was fertile ground for their cause. Lucille and Suzanne walked towards the vehicles parked next to the cemetery. They avoided the hearse and walked from the back of the line forward. Many windows were open to air out the cars; they surreptitiously dropped paper wads through these windows and moved up the line. When they felt themselves getting too conspicuous, they walked into the cemetery proper, joining other curious civilians, and stood through the ceremony. It was a brilliantly sunny day; the enlisted men, already in a state of poor morale, were given permission to remove their coats, and they slung them over their arms. The two women walked by the clusters of men standing at parade rest, brushing by their coats, slipping wads of paper into the occasional exposed pocket. They kept a sombre expression on their faces to blend in with the expressions of the other attendees. When those assembled began to sing *'Deutschland, Deutschland über Alles'*, they gave each other sly looks and muttered curses. Most of the other civilians looked equally uncomfortable, and left as soon as the song was over.

After the young enlisted men were marched away, and the officers headed for their cars, Suzanne and Lucille hung back, slowing their steps until the Germans were gone and the other onlookers had dispersed. They stopped outside the little fisherman's chapel to share a cigarette.

'Well, *cherie*,' said Suzanne, 'they continue to commit suicide. I regret the loss of life, but I think it is a good sign, don't you?'

'Well, if what we heard on the BBC is true, the war is not going our way yet. But if they are already committing suicide, things are bad for them, and will get worse.'

'I suppose no army ever lost because of many suicides, though?'

'No, *cherie*, I am not aware of any.' They gazed out to the sea for a silent minute. 'But it shows that we are not here for retirement, but once again for the advance of revolution and freedom. We are not old aunties yet!' Lucille coughed as she chuckled and exhaled, and handed Suzanne the cigarette.

Suddenly they were startled by the chapel door opening. Suzanne dropped the cigarette. A bedraggled young woman emerged, pushing a bicycle.

CHAPTER 10

Nantes, France

Lucy Schwob had started life in Nantes with words on her side. She was doted on by her father, a newspaper editor, and her uncle Marcel, a writer. She was a very intelligent little girl with curly blonde hair and deep blue eyes. Hers was a wealthy literary family with a passion for words and truth. Books dominated the décor; poets and playwrights of the avant garde threw grapes at one another at the dining table. Lucy's mother's growing madness, her gradual slipping-away from reason, was all the more painful for this. Gradually, her mother developed complete disregard for the beauty of words, and turned the idea of symbols into weapons to use against the world. Maurice Schwob tried to ignore it, then to keep it a secret. His despair grew as his wife's behaviour became more bizarre. When they were speaking English on holidays in England, she stopped using the word 'go': 'I am coming to the shore,' 'You need to come to school soon,' 'The hot weather is coming away.' Nobody said anything. When would four-year-old Lucille notice? Actually, she already had. She began by trying to fix her mother. 'It's not "come", it's "go", stop saying "come".' Her mother ignored her.

Back in Nantes, her mother spoke French in equally bizarre fashion. Often she would cut some obscure article out of the newspaper, something about farming or cattle exports, and show it to her husband, waiting for him to grasp its significance. Something was wrong, wrong, wrong. Lucy tried being extra-good. Her father tried courtesy, reasoning, pleading.

Articles on peach hybridisation and bridge repairs were left on his breakfast plate. Lucy was puzzled, then terrified, as her mother began accusing Lucy of having 'friends' who stole household items and turned Lucy against her. Lucy stopped eating, began hiding in her room, picking at her scalp until it bled. Her mother would fly into rages, shouting at her, 'Don't you know I'm the best mother in the world?' Lucy's eyes would fill with tears, her nails would tear at her scalp. She was beginning to hate her mother, and she knew that was bad. She was a bad girl who made her mother talk funny. She started lecturing her dolls on good behaviour, hurling the ones who wouldn't pay attention against the wall.

She loved her father. She could tell him. One day as the two of them were going to see his mother in the Cambronne apartment building, she said, 'Papa, I don't like *Maman*. She's bad to me. '

His head whipped around. 'What do you mean?'

'She shouts at me and says I have friends who do things to her. Papa, I don't have any friends! Nobody plays with me! I'm a bad girl.She says I'm bad all the time!'

He looked down at his little girl, who looked up at him with complete trust, but also with anger, demanding that he understand her. She was thin and pale, with dirty, even bloody, fingernails. Her blonde curls looked patchy. But it was her gaze that unnerved him the most; he would never forget it. He turned his head away and composed himself. This wave of strange behaviour had so depleted his ability to cope, he had not noticed what was happening to his daughter.

'Sweetheart, you are a very GOOD girl. *Maman* cannot help it.'

'Yes, she can, Papa. I tell her to, but she doesn't listen to me.'

'Lucy, do you love your grandmother?'

'Yes, I love *Mamé*. She gives me biscuits and little cups of tea, and we make up plays with all my dolls. Don't be angry with me for drinking tea, Papa!' She began to cry.

'No, no, *cherie*. It is all right. I am not angry with you for anything.'

'You aren't?'

'Lucy, what if you stayed with *Mamé* for a while until *Maman* feels better?'

'Would you visit me?'

'Oh, of course I would.'

'I would like to stay at *Mamé*'s house, then.' She tilted her little face to him with such a look of relief, he burst into tears and hugged her.

CHAPTER 11

St Brelade, Jersey

Spring 1941

'Excuse me,' Marlene muttered, as if she were passing them in a shop aisle. They were two middle-aged ladies, one short and one tall and somewhat stolid. They looked dressed up for some occasion. She pushed the bicycle a few steps as they looked on, momentarily speechless.

'Not at all,' said a bemused Lucille with a smirk. 'I do hope we did not disturb you.' She instantly regretted her remark when she saw the look of hurt on Marlene's face. Before Marlene could say something, she said, '*Cherie*, are you all right? Were you hiding from the German boy's funeral? Did you know him?'

This only served to distress her more. 'What boy? I don't know any Germans! I don't know what they're doing here! I … ' She put up a hand to her eyes but the tears had already begun to roll down her cheeks.

Suzanne gave Lucille a disapproving glance, all too familiar with her tendency towards tactlessness. Lucille bit her lip as Suzanne approached Marlene, who looked twice as bedraggled as she had a minute before. Suzanne placed her hand on Marlene's, which gripped the handlebar weakly.

'*Cherie*,' she said, 'please excuse us. We did not intend to hurt your feelings.'

Marlene shook her head, unable to speak.

'Please come and have some tea with us. If you do not want to talk about your troubles, that is all right, but perhaps we can help you.'

This brought forth more sobs from Marlene, but they discerned the word 'job' in her outpouring. They looked at each other, knowing that they trusted this woman and were going to help her. Now Lucille approached her.

'Come, *cherie*, please have some tea with us and tell us your story.'

Marlene nodded and they set off.

La Rocquaise was dilapidated and adorned with photographs and paintings the likes of which Marlene had never seen. Women with large heads squishing out of tiny bodies, naked men, breasts surrounding eyeballs. A man-about-town leaning on a mantel, a kneeling Buddha, a woman in eighteenth-century costume, a woman holding a bar-bell and wearing a leotard emblazoned with 'I am in training don't kiss me'. Fashion watercolours from the 1920s with gamines in costume, cigarettes drooping languidly from red lips, adorned a separate wall. Only later would Marlene realise that all the photographs were of Lucille, and all the watercolours by Suzanne. Although the images were unnerving, she was quickly made to feel at home by the women's hospitality and solicitude.

Suzanne set down a strangely ornate coffee pot and poured parsnip 'coffee' (if you put it in a teapot it would be parsnip 'tea', really tasting like neither) and sliced heavy potato 'bread'. She had changed into a smock-like garment and trousers, which Marlene found quite strange. Her hair was now dark brown, as if it had been transplanted from Lucille's head to her own. Lucille, on the other hand, now sported short dyed-red hair that somehow complemented her wine-coloured dress. She was pale, with piercing eyes and a nose in the shape of a semicircle. She was quite animated, circling around Suzanne in a bird-like manner and chattering with her and, occasionally, with Marlene. Her hands fluttered about as she talked, and Marlene sat a little distance from her when she saw her gesturing a little too carelessly with a lighted cigarette.

Marlene was pleased to realise that the reward for the risk she had taken was to meet these people, far more interesting than the girls from the office. The women seemed to like her, and when she accepted their offer of lodging and a job they quickly negotiated an agreement. Marlene would work their kitchen garden, plus whatever other rows she could till. In return, they would hide her, using both the walls around the compound and their talent for disguise. This was a good arrangement for Lucille and Suzanne, who were used to city life and who found that the creeping joint stiffness and other maladies of middle age were obstacles to their reinventing themselves completely as farmers.

Before the weather warmed, Marlene planted beans and lettuce as well as swedes. The ladies bartered some wine for a chicken; the resulting eggs were a welcome addition to their meals and also were excellent bribery material. Marlene carried at least two eggs on her at all times in case anyone should show too much curiosity about her identity. So far, nobody had. Nonetheless, the ladies decided that she should shave her head and wear one of Lucille's huge collection of wigs, changing them often so that it looked as if one drudge after another was tilling their soil.

Marlene had explained to them about her card, and Miss Viner's; they had heartily approved. One morning, the three sat at the dining-room table after a breakfast of swedes, peas and a single egg divided three ways. Lucille spoke up.

'As you know, we write letters to the soldiers encouraging them to mutiny. We do not wish to ask you to help us in this unless you know the risks and wish to take them. You have already done so much, you do not have to do any more if you do not want to.'

Both women looked at her. Marlene twisted her calloused hands in her lap.

'No, I want to do more, *mademoiselles*. Please don't worry. I understand the risks. Besides, they don't know who I am, do they?'

'We do not know that, *cherie*. It is unwise to assume.'

'Well, anyway, what did you want to do?'

'We want to go into St Helier and give out more letters. We also hear that some citizens are turning in others as black marketeers, or as Jews. We need to stop them.'

'How will you do that?'

'We have some ideas. One way is to inform on them. Falsely, of course, but it will get them out of the way for a while.'

'I see.'

'Do you wish to go with us?'

Marlene thought of Mr Orange's officious manner, Pauline's salacious giggle, of poor Mr Davidson and the others who had registered and were now living in terror.

'Yes, I'll go.'

'*Très bien*! We will have fun! Let us select our disguises!'

'I need to wear my coat.'

'Why, *cherie*?'

'Because it has important things sewn into it.'

'Oh, you are a very smart young woman, Marlene! But of course you shall wear your coat. This is a dangerous undertaking. You must understand that if any one of us is caught, she will be tortured!'

'I wouldn't tell them anything!'

Suzanne answered, her brow furrowed. 'No, *cherie*. It is not right. We do not want you to be tortured. They are evil, evil men. They are filthy swine who will do anything to a young girl to get information. Plus, if they think you are a Jew, they will be even more beastly. They will torture you, get information out of you, and then kill you or drive you to kill yourself. Please understand, Lucille and I have many plans for any eventuality. If one of us is captured, the other will be able to get away.' She said this with her characteristic nonchalance, but Marlene could see her hands shaking.

Lucille came over to Suzanne's chair and squeezed her shoulders. '*Cherie*, let us not dwell on unpleasantness. We will be fine. Marlene will be fine. We must – '

'No, no, Lucille. You are right. There is no time for silliness. There is only time to fight the enemy, may he rot in hell.'

Thirty minutes later they were pedalling single-file (the Nazis forbade riding two or more abreast) down the coastal road. Marlene had a garish red wig secured to her bald head; a chartreuse scarf trailed behind her. She had an off-white light woollen dress underneath her coat, heavy stockings and sensible shoes. With a smear of red lipstick and a silly little hat, she looked like an older woman making a pathetic attempt to look younger; she was certain nobody would bother her. Indeed, nobody had ever bothered her when she was a young woman; now it mattered not at all and instead was a distinct advantage. She felt so serious and so lighthearted at the same time.

Lucille and Suzanne were so generous, so funny. She had never met anyone like them before. Then again, she had never known any artists. They actually had ideas and acted on them. Even when they were putting themselves in the greatest danger they were aware of beauty. She now saw their house as beautiful. Billows of interesting fabric framed the windows.

47

Their plates were hand-painted in fanciful ways; Lucille said some of the decorations were 'Cubist'. Flying down the road, Marlene inhaled lungfuls of air, not to calm herself as she had when pedalling the opposite way a month ago, but to fill herself with the energy to fight.

CHAPTER 12

Nantes

Lucy's mother, raving about lanterns in the cellar, was reluctantly sent off to a Parisian clinic for a short visit. She was to return to the clinic often, for longer and longer stays. Lucy remained with her grandmother, Mathilde Cahun, until she was ten. Her gaze never softened; deprived of a mother's frame of reference, she regarded the world with a fierce curiosity, without assumptions. At the same time, she valued her dream life as much as her waking life, recording her dreams and pondering them, seriously regarding their ideas. She excelled in school; the other children were afraid of her. This fear changed to hostility when she was twelve and Dreyfus was again in the news. Her defiant gaze was not enough to deflect the onslaught of insults and taunts. Her father found her an English tutor. She settled into the flowered parlour at Parson's Mead in Surrey and astonished Miss Henry with her grasp of English literature and art. On a visit, her father gave her a camera. At first, she tried to suck the world in with it. Then, she realised it was an extension of her mind. The little cables and timers she discovered enabled her to give form to her dreams by making self-portraits.

A year later, back in Nantes, her father encouraged her new pursuit, though he had hoped it would lead to her getting more fresh air, rather than further closeting herself in her room. It took her a while, then, to notice her father's more frequent absences. She was studying beauty. Women's beauty held special allure for her. She tried making herself as beautiful as possible, like the dancer (and lover of King Leopold) Cléo de Merode, but the face in the resulting photograph seemed masked. Afraid of misrepresenting her soul, she began to wear more simple and severe clothing, sometimes approaching male dress. She was pleased with the resulting photographs; the mask of gender was lifted somehow, the gaze more meaningful.

She tried fuelling her dreams with ether. The visions were astounding, sometimes terrifying, with monsters cascading down mountains of yellow fire, exploding into flaming debris. Was she tempting madness? Should she die? A few cuts to her wrists and some deep intoxications brought no answers. Her father tried ceaselessly to reconnect her to the world while respecting her dreams.

At dinner one evening her father, who had separated from her mother (but still paid all her hospital bills), turned to fifteen-year-old Lucille with a piece of bread in his hand.

'Would you like to go on an outing to the zoo on Sunday? I wish you to meet someone.'

'Who?'

'A lady, a … widow, I … er … have become … friends with. She has a daughter a couple of years older than you named Suzanne. She will come, too.'

'Are you going to marry this lady?' Her gaze went through him; he put the bread down.

'I might. But I want you to meet her and her daughter first.'

'All right, I'll go on Sunday.'

Suzanne. Does she dream? Does she wear masks? Has she begun to menstruate? Does she cry for her father?

They would laugh later on about their meeting in front of the fetid monkey cage. Each briefly assessed, and found acceptable, the other's parent. Then they trained their eyes on each other.

50

Suzanne was taller, older, darker. She had a languid gaze that made Lucy shiver when it was turned upon her. The little foursome commenced walking through the zoo, the older man and woman in front, arm in arm, chatting and laughing; the young women behind, interviewing each other for the job of sister. Each expected rejection from the other due to her affinity for dreams; they were overjoyed to find how much they actually shared.

'You have a dream book, too?'

'Yes.'

'What does it look like?'

'It is a notebook with a tiger on the cover.'

'Mine has a jungle flower. My father gave it to me. Suzanne, have you ever tried ether?'

'No, but I would like to. I hear the dreams are exquisite.'

'I have used it. It's wonderful, although it gives you a headache later.'

'Have you ever tried to kill yourself?'

'Yes, when my dreams became too big for me.'

'I tried when my father was dying. I'm glad they found me.'

'Me, too. So, do you like to paint?'

'No, I draw. My dream book has more pages of drawings than writing.'

'I don't draw. I do photography. I haven't tried illustrating my dream book, but you are giving me ideas.'

Over dinner in a café they were more like two couples than two families tentatively meeting. Lucille's father and Suzanne's mother were relieved that their precocious, bohemian daughters got along so well. The older couple spoke of food, literature and politics. The younger spoke of dreams.

There was no rush to marriage for Maurice Schwob and Marie Eugénie Malherbe; Maurice's divorce from Lucy's mother would take years. They enjoyed each other's company and spent time at each other's homes. The girls each had a guest bedroom at the other's house. At the Schwob home, they changed this to a shared bedroom and a studio for drawing and photography. Their parents were delighted over their friendship; both girls seemed much happier and less crushed by the world; their parents willingly supplied paper, books, and lenient bedtimes. Lucy and Suzanne began to frequent artists' cafés, where they read their experimental poetry, shared their drawings and photographs, drank glass after glass of wine, and tumbled into their beds to get some rest before school. It was only natural that they should become lovers; they were already finishing each other's sentences. One night, as they were sitting on Suzanne's bed in their shared room, reading Rimbaud, Suzanne started to drowse.

'Are you sleepy?'

'Just a little.'

'Shall I tuck you in and kiss you goodnight?'

'Yes.'

Lucille eased Suzanne down onto her bed, pulled the covers out from under her legs, covered her, and kissed her goodnight. Then she kissed her some more; Suzanne murmured her pleasure. Lucille got under the covers, held the now wide-awake Suzanne, and covered her face with more kisses, which were soon fervently returned. Buttons were undone, breasts caressed, nipples kissed into hardness. Hands sought out soft bellies and then, frantic with desire, the known-yet-unknown territory of lusciousness below. They became thunderclouds, merging in softness and seething electricity. After, they clung together, giggling, weeping, kissing.

CHAPTER 13

Jersey

26 April 1941

```
THIRD ORDER
relating to measures against Jews
```

In virtue of the plenary powers conferred upon me
by the Führer and Supreme Commander of the
Wehrmacht, I order as follows:

§ 1. Jews
(1) Any person having at least three
grand-parents of pure Jewish blood shall be
deemed to be a Jew. A grand-parent having
belonged to the Jewish religious community shall
be deemed to be of pure Jewish blood.
  Any person having two grand-parents of pure
Jewish blood who —

    (a) at the time of the publication of this
        Order, belongs to the Jewish religious
        community or who subsequently joins it; or
    (b) at the time of the publication of this
        Order is married to a Jew or who
        subsequently marries a Jew;

shall be deemed to be a Jew.
  In doubtful cases, any person who belongs or
has belonged to the Jewish religious community
shall be deemed to be a Jew.

(2) § 1 of the Order of September 27, 1940,
relating to measures against Jews (Official
Orders of the Military Commander in France
(VOBIF), page 92) is hereby revoked.

§ 2. Subsequent Declaration.
(1) Any person, not having previously been deemed

to be a Jew, who comes within the terms of §1 of this Order, shall, in accordance with §3 of the Order of September 27, 1940, relating to measures against Jews (VOBIF p. 92) and with §§ 2 and 3 of the Second Order of October 18th, 1940, relating to measures against Jews (VOBIF p.112), make the required declaration before May 20th, 1941.

(2) Measures against persons, having previously been deemed to be Jews, who do not come within the terms of § 1 of this Order, shall be withdrawn on request.

§ 3. Prohibition on the carrying-on of certain economic activities and on the employment of Jews. (1) On and after May 20th, 1941, Jews and Jewish undertakings for whom or for which a managing administrator has not been appointed shall be prohibited from carrying on the following economic activities:

    (a) wholesale and retail trade;
    (b) hotel and catering industry;
    (c) insurance;
    (d) navigation;
    (e) dispatch and storage;
    (f) travel agencies, organisation of tours;
    (g) guides;
    (h) transport undertakings of all descriptions, including the hire of motor and other vehicles;
    (i) banking & money-exchange;
    (j) pawnbroking;
    (k) information and money-collecting offices;
    (l) supervision undertakings;
    (m) dealings in automatic machines;
    (n) publicity agencies;
    (o) employment agencies;
    (p) businesses concerned with dealings in apartments, lands, and mortgages;
    (q) matrimonial agencies;
    (r) intermediaries for dealings in goods and industrial loans (agents, brokers, representatives, travellers, etc.).

(2) In no undertaking shall a Jew be engaged as a higher official or as an employee who comes into contact with customers. Persons who alone or jointly with others have right of signature or who have an interest in the profits of the undertaking or who individually are designated as such by the Military Commander or the competent French authorities shall be deemed to be higher officials.

(3) On the order of the Military Commander or the competent French authorities, Jewish employees shall be dismissed and replaced by non-Jewish employees.

§ 4. Holdings and Shares belonging to Jews.
   Managing administrators may be appointed to administer holdings in limited liability companies and shares belonging to Jews and Jewish undertakings. The provisions of the Order of May 20th, 1940, on the management of businesses (VOBIF p. 31) shall apply accordingly to managing administrators. Managing administrators are authorised to sell holdings and shares. They shall have, with regard to the company, the same rights as the owners of the holdings or shares.

§ 5. Indispensable advances.
   Until further orders, managing administrators of Jewish undertakings, holdings or shares shall not advance to the persons entitled to the same, out of the management income, more than is absolutely indispensable.

§ 6. Compensation.
(1) No compensation shall be awarded for losses resulting from the carrying into effect of the Orders relating to measures against Jews.

(2) Jewish employees who are dismissed as from May 1st, 1941, or any later date, despite the fact that their employment is not prohibited, shall not be entitled to claim compensation for dismissal without due notice.

§ 7. Penalties.
Infringements of this Order shall be punishable by imprisonment and a fine or either of these penalties, unless a more severe penalty is otherwise prescribed.
Confiscation of goods may also be ordered.

§ 8. Commencement.
This Order shall come into force as from its publication.

The Military Commander in France.

CHAPTER 14

St Helier, Jersey

27 April 1941

They sat in the little kitchen, drinking precious tea. They were in the home of Mary Drummond, a postal worker in St Helier. After checking for busybodies at the windows, Mary took out a large envelope and emptied its contents on the table. It was a sheaf of letters, all addressed to the *Feldkommandantur* from Islanders. Mary had smuggled them out of the post office before they reached their destination. The sisters began reading them; Marlene followed suit. They told of this person hoarding coal, that person selling butter on the black market, that one with Jewish ancestry who was 'passing' as an Aryan.

Mary looked grim. 'So many,' she said. 'It's getting worse.'

Marlene was shocked. 'Aren't these people neighbours? Why are they doing this?'

Mary, a widow in her fifties, smiled maternally at Marlene. 'Dear, most of these charges are false. They just want to settle scores.'

'It's a shame,' sighed Lucille. 'Such *petit bourgeois* behaviour.'

Lucille and Suzanne took out a box of mixed stationery unlike the fancy paper they used to write letters to soldiers. This was a collection of various cheap lined papers and prosaic light-blue, deckle-edge bond. Mary produced three typewriters. They began typing letters, similar to those they were perusing, but naming the authors as the suspects. These were put into envelopes addressed to the *Feldkommandantur*, to be posted at various points on the island.

Then they set off for a stroll around St Helier, avoiding areas Marlene used to frequent, though nobody would have recognised her in her disguise. Nobody would probably recognise me even without a disguise, thought Marlene. Was I ever Miss Popular? Did I ever have many friends? Would they have ever found out my father was Jewish if Pauline and her bloody jerry hadn't seen me at the cemetery? What has become of my flat? Who lives there now? Do they think I'm dead? Curiosity about such things aside, she realised that she didn't miss her former existence much. Instead of working in a boring office with girls much younger than herself and a boss who listened to Lord Haw-Haw, she was out in the fresh air. She was meeting people who talked about things like freedom and victory and beauty instead of film stars and boyfriends and hosiery. The sisters were very kind and funny, though a little strange. Mary Drummond was a pleasant woman; Marlene began to reflect on her incredible bravery, doing something on a daily basis that had so frightened Marlene that she had left her own workplace after stealing only two documents. How did Mary smuggle out so much post addressed to the *Feldkommandantur* and not die of a nervous breakdown? Mary certainly seemed a bit fatigued and put-upon, as everyone else did in these times, but she had a matter-of-fact cheerfulness that Marlene envied. It reminded Marlene of her mother. What would her mother think of her now? She suppressed a smile.

They rounded a corner. Across the street several young women were strolling and looking in the shop windows. One was tall, with red hair. Marlene recognised Pauline and began to tremble.

'We need to find a café,' Suzanne was saying. 'We have notes for the soldiers.'

Mary and Lucille began discussing this, trying to decide

which café might actually have something edible and also have a German clientèle sympathetic to their message. Marlene did not hear them; she froze momentarily in her tracks, then turned her head away from the street and hurried to catch up with the three women.

'Are you all right, *cherie*?' asked Lucille.

'Did you see something?'

'I saw someone.'

'Whom?'

'The woman who informed on me. She saw me at the Jewish cemetery and told my boss.'

'Oh, the little bitch!' cried Lucille. 'Do not worry. We will protect you. Are you sure?'

'Yes,' Marlene said, trying to stop shaking.

They stopped at a café frequented by German soldiers. They ordered an expensive pot of tea, took out their bread (the café having nothing to eat), and managed to chitchat long enough that the other diners stopped paying attention to them. As they left, they dropped a note from the Nameless Soldier on an adjoining empty table, and dropped two crumpled ones into the pockets of soldiers' coats draped on the backs of chairs. They took a roundabout route back to Mary's house, dropping a letter or two into each postbox on the way. They picked up their bicycles and set off for St Brelade in the late afternoon. Marlene had not had so much tea in weeks, and was still very nervous. The sighting of Pauline had undone any benefit afforded by weeks of work outdoors.

Back at home, the women plied her with cognac and questions. Was Pauline a jerrybag? Well, yes. She had seen her with a soldier. Did Pauline still work in the Aliens Office? She didn't know. What was Pauline's last name? Barrett.

A letter was quickly drafted, on the cheap lined paper,

naming Pauline as a black marketeer. 'She will go to the prison in Lille,' chuckled Suzanne, 'a little vacation from her busy activities as an informant.'

Churchill held forth on the wireless that night, extolling the bravery and cheerfulness of the British citizenry he had encountered. 'What a proof of the virtues of free institutions; what a test of the quality of our local authorities ... ' Yes, what a test indeed, mused Marlene bitterly, thinking of Pauline and Mr Orange. He went on, talking about the German invasion of Greece, which was battling Italy: 'Meanwhile, Hitler ... suddenly made it clear that he would come to the rescue of his fellow-criminal ... While nearly all the Greek troops were busy beating the Italians, the tremendous German military machine suddenly towered up on their other frontier. In their mortal peril, the Greeks turned to us for succour. Strained as were our own resources, we could not say them "nay" ... There are rules against that kind of thing, and to break those rules would be fatal to the honour of the British Empire, without which we could neither hope, nor deserve, to win this hard war ... ' His comments on Britain's refusal to abandon Greece in her time of need went over Marlene's head, but the sisters looked at each other and nodded at this posthumous dig at Chamberlain.

CHAPTER 15

No. 1, F.B. Cottages

Greve d'Azette

10 June 1941

Dear Sir,

I am in doubt as to whether the new order
relating to Jews affects myself or not, and would
be most grateful if you will kindly inform me
what to do about registering, I am the wife of
Leonard Charles ISAAC's (at present out of the
island) who is a Jew on the paternal side but not
on the maternal side, he was baptised Church of
England and as far as I know has never BELONGED
to any Jewish religion, not being a Jewess myself
I do not think the order concerns me, but will
feel more satisfied on receiving your advice.

I remain,
Yours truly,
Ada Isaacs (née RIGBY)

CHAPTER 16

France

'Uranian' was a term for it, taken from the writings of Plato. Havelock Ellis, whom Lucille would later translate into French, called it 'sexual inversion', and mentioned its association with free and creative minds. When their parents finally married in 1917, when Lucille was 23, Lucille and Suzanne moved into a fourth-floor apartment in the headquarters of *Phare de la Loire*, Lucille's father's newspaper. They had begun to acquire literary reputations, having written and illustrated for *Phare*, as well as for the more avant-garde *Le Mercure de France*. The following year, Lucille began studies at the Sorbonne, and they threw themselves into the literary and artistic life of Paris. Lucille settled on the name Claude Cahun, continued to write, and then took up her camera again. Suzanne became Marcel Moore, illustrator. They were young, smart, well-off and talented. Claude shaved her head, created more self-portraits. She began to realise the inadvertent gift of her mother: she had never known what 'normal' was. The blessing of uncertainty bestowed on a brilliant mind was the source of her power.

One Christmas she gave Marcel a poem about Heaven as a trap for men. Why not regard Heaven with uncertainty? Had anyone thought about it? 'Nothing is easier than to enter into Paradise; but – believe the experience of a prisoner – if you pass the threshold, you will not exit! ... And you will never know the voluptuous Hell, the varied Hell, the seven season

Hell, with unforeseen Springs, where each chooses his own hour; the only place which resembles and brings back to the Earth – the brothel of the Eternal.'

CHAPTER 17

Le Masurier, Giffard & Poch
23 Hill Street

Jersey, June 13th. 1941

Clifford Orange, Esq.
Chief Aliens Officer
Hill Street,
Jersey

Dear Sir,

Third Order relating to Measures against Jews.

Mrs Catherine Pauline Hill (née Jacobs)

We beg to acknowledge receipt of your letter of
the 11th. instant.
  We regret that we have been unable to ascertain
any facts which have given rise to the
supposition that Mrs. Hill is a Jewess.
  We thought it our duty, when you wrote on the
23rd. November last, to inform you that we were
acting for Mrs. Hill, whose maiden name was
Jacobs. Apart from the fact that the surname
Jacobs may be of Jewish origin, which was the
sole reason which led us to suppose that our
client might possibly be a Jewess, we knew of
nothing which might help to prove that she was,
in fact, a Jewess.
  Perhaps we may add that Mrs. Hill was the wife
of Mr. Walter Albert Russell Hill, who was
formerly the owner of the Halkett Hotel.
  We have every reason to believe that Mr. Hill
was an Aryan.

Yours faithfully,
Le Masurier, Giffard & Poch.

```
================================================
```

Field Command 515

[Translation]

4th July 1941

The Bailiff of Jersey

Official Journal No. 36, dated 10th June 1941

```
================================================
```

The fourth Order concerning anti-Jewish measures
dated 28th May need not be published and
registered. I request you, however, to bring it
to the attention of the representative of
Commercial Properties, Ltd. [owned by Phineas
Cohen, removed to London]. The approval required
in accordance with paragraphs 1 and 2 is, in case
of necessity, to be obtained from the Field
Command.

For the Field Commander,
von Stein, O.K.V.R.

CHAPTER 18

St Brelade, Jersey

July 1941

Marlene, Lucille and Suzanne had heard it on the BBC. 'The night is your friend, and "V" is your sign.' The Morse code for the letter 'V' was played on a drum and then followed by the first four notes of Beethoven's Fifth Symphony, whose *dit-dit-dit-da* were the same tempo. They set out at night with sticks of chalk, writing 'V' on walls and in the streets. They smuggled folded-up 'V's to funerals, dropping them into cars and pockets. Suzanne and Lucille laughed at Bailiff Carey's announcement of a fine for anyone caught making the letter. It frightened Marlene, though; what side was he on? Was he, as well as Mr Orange, going over to the Germans? Were they only concerned about avoiding retribution? Not that there hadn't been any. Wireless sets were confiscated within a certain radius of sites where people were caught painting 'V's. They were later returned, but it put people out. Well, running away from her job and home in St Helier had certainly put Marlene out, hadn't it? The people required to put 'Jewish Undertaking' signs in their windows, and then ordered to auction off their businesses in the spring, were put out, weren't they? Who was putting us out the most? The Germans! Marlene sliced some swedes for lunch; she could not fashion artistic shapes out of them so just made thin rounds. She cut a half slice of rationed bread for each person. They had parsnip coffee with a little milk in it. Lucille noted Marlene's angry expression as they began their meal.

'What is it, Marlene?'

'Nothing, Lucille.'

'No, dear Marlene, you are upset. What is it?'

'Everything.' She put her fork down and rubbed her brow.

'We know, Marlene. You are a very brave young woman. We still have our home; you have left yours. *Cherie*, you do not have to go with us on all our resistance missions. You have more at risk, although we are Jewish, too.'

'What?'

'Yes, *cherie*, we are Jews.'

'But you didn't register.'

They both laughed. 'Marlene,' said Suzanne, squeezing Marlene's hand, 'we do not comply with the government in many ways. Remember, we were revolutionaries in Paris. We are still revolutionaries in love!'

Suzanne put her free hand around Lucille's shoulders and gave her a hug. Marlene vaguely understood what Suzanne was saying; she had noticed they often shared a bedroom, but she never asked them about it. What business was it of hers?

Suzanne continued. 'We grew up in Jewish families, but we did not go to the synagogue. The Nazis do not ask you if you went to synagogue or not. They hate all Jews, as you know.'

'Yes.'

'It is perhaps foolish of us to expect you to come with us on all our escapades. We are older. You have more to lose.'

Marlene found herself shouting. 'No!' she said. 'I want to come with you! What kind of life do I have ahead of me? I'm a bloody old maid!' She immediately felt badly after she said it; she worried Lucille and Suzanne would be offended. Instead, they chuckled.

Lucille spoke up. '*Mais non*! You are a revolutionary hero- ine! You have already saved one woman from the Germans by destroying her card! You are braver than many men! *Cherie*, you shall have many lovers!'

Marlene felt her cheeks burning; the women laughed harder.

'I have never had a lover.' Marlene pressed her lips together. There was a brief silence.

'You shall,' said Lucille with amusing certainty. 'When this war is over, we will take you to Paris. It will be like it was in the old days, before Pétain and all the fascists.'

Suzanne broke in. 'Listen to my *optimiste*! Shall I pack a valise? Will the war be over next week?'

Lucille would have none of her sarcasm. 'No, we must believe! Every Monday, I think the war will end on Friday. The more "V"s we paint, the more letters the Soldier Without a Name writes, the sooner that Friday will come. What do you think, Marlene?'

Marlene could not bear to disagree with Lucille. 'Yes, you are right. If not this Friday, then the Friday after. I want to go to Paris!'

'You have never been there?' Lucille looked shocked.

'No, I haven't. I have never been anywhere.'

'Not to the other Islands?'

'I went to Sark once, with my school. That is all.'

'You poor little chick. It is too bad that the war has been the only thing to bring you excitement.'

'This is excitement I can do without, thank you very much!'

They laughed. Lucille grabbed her 'coffee' and held the cup aloft. 'To victory!'

'To victory!' toasted Marlene and Suzanne. They drained their cups.

CHAPTER 19

Paris

They tried to create in an ossifying Paris. Claude penned 'Uranian Games', replete with startling imagery of sexual ambiguity, nurturing and death: 'I hide within him and I look at you from beneath his eyelids. How would I have a name, a body, an idea of my own, I, his pale reflection, the shadow which follows him word by word? What am I, if not the friend of my friend?'

She wrote of Biblical heroines; of Judith walking to the enemy camp with a rescued baby bird under her arm, it starting out 'warmer than my feverish armpit', then cooling and dying there. Was it the death of innocence, or the banishment of sentimentality? In 'Games', she wrote of Marcel holding tightly to a tiny bat, representing negative ideas, eventually releasing but remembering it. They closed the decade with *Aveux non Avenues*, a book of photomontages, images of people and parts of people arranged into stylised mandalas; Claude's head turned inside out and placed on paper like a map.

With the Thirties came little relief for the disabled veterans, the bitter widows, the man-empty towns left behind by the Great War. The Depression eventually hit and found France's serial governments unprepared. The pacifism of the Twenties hardened into isolationism.

People ran to align themselves with the various flavours of fascism: the Parti Populaire Française, Parti Social Français, the Action Française. Not content with his fortune from perfume, François Coty had launched an anti-Semitic daily, *L'Ami du Peuple*, which boasted three million readers by 1930.

Claude and Marcel were welcomed into André Breton's Surrealist sphere, which disdained snob art and oppression, religion, mysticism and the over-serious. Feelings and dreams were important; hysteria but another form of expression. They posed the awesome threat of the Other; the middle finger stuck up in the face of Authority. After all, if singing the 'wrong' song or having the 'wrong' penis could land you in trouble, making a picture of a woman with two heads was as dangerous as throwing a Molotov cocktail. Several Surrealists were to die in the camps; several Japanese artists were imprisoned.

The Thirties lurched on. Franco crushed the Republicans. Hitler reoccupied the Rhineland. Claude and Marcel wrote, photographed, drew. They also affixed their signatures to an anti-Nazi declaration, and took the step of buying the house in St Brelade, installing a large photography studio. If Paris was unrecognisable now, ready to spit them out like rotten fruit, they needed a place to land.

'Claude' and 'Marcel' changed back to 'Lucille' and 'Suzanne' when they moved to Jersey in May of 1938 to live quietly together, making soldier dolls out of newspaper and photographing them in the sand. Again, a bird died under their arms. The diamond glint of the sun on the Bay and the antics of the gulls were lost on them as they paced the floor and listened to Western Europe capitulate to Germany's demand for the Sudetenland, then held each other and wept as they heard France fall. Resistance work was the only possible choice.

CHAPTER 20

13 August 1941

```
Mrs. A Isaacs,
1, F.B. Cottages,
Greve d'Azette,
St. Clement,
Jersey

Third Order relating to measures against Jews

Madam,

I am directed to inform you that it has been
finally established that you are not a Jewess
under the terms of the Third Jewish Order, dated
26th. April, 1941.

I am, Madam,
Your obedient servant,

Clifford Orange
Chief Aliens Officer.


==============================================


Field Command 515

[Translation]

2nd September 1941

The Bailiff of Jersey

Official Journal No. 39, dated 22nd August 1941.

1. The Third Order for the execution and
amendment of the Order concerning property, dated
```

31st July 1941, need be neither published nor registered.

2. The Order concerning the confiscation of wireless sets of Jews must either be registered and published in German and English or all Jews must be notified individually.

For the Field Commander,
Dr. Brosch, K.V.R.

==

Aliens Office,
Jersey

11th September 1941.

The Bailiff of Jersey.

Order concerning the withdrawal of Wireless Sets of Jews, dated 13th August, 1941.

Sir,

I have the honour to refer to your Memorandum (W30/66) of the 5th. instant regarding the above Order and to report that three Wireless Sets have been deposited with me at this Office by the following registered Jews:-

1. Mr. Hyam Goldman,
Milestone Cottage,
St. Peter's Valley.

2. Mr. John Jacobs,
4, St. Clement's Gardens
St. Clement's.

3. Mr. Nathan Davidson,
59 Oxford Road,
St. Helier.

Each Jew, whose name is contained in the Jewish
Register, has been interviewed by me, in person,
and the remainder, eight in number, have stated
that they do not possess Wireless Sets. A record
of their statements has been kept in my file.

I have the honour to be, Sir,
Your obedient servant,

Clifford Orange
Chief Aliens Officer

==

Fifth Order relating to measures against the Jews

VOIBF p. 297

September 28, 1941

In virtue of the plenary powers conferred upon me
by the Führer and Supreme Commander of the
Wehrmacht, I order as follows:

§ 1
Administrators of Jewish undertakings shall, at
the termination of their management, deposit 90%
of the net proceeds with the Jersey Department of
Finance and Economics. The other 10% shall be
deposited in the account of the General
Commissioner for the Jewish Question. Only the
absolute indispensable amount shall be disbursed
to the Jewish associate.

§ 2
This is in keeping with § 4 of the Fourth Order
relating to measures against the Jews.

§ 3
This Order shall be submitted for publication.

The Military Commander in France

CHAPTER 21

Cherbourg

December 1941

Rain lashed the thirty prisoners' faces as they were herded aboard the lurching vessel. LeBlanc, the little Vichy shit, shouted at them to hurry. Before they had been soldiers, then refugees, then detainees, now prisoners. Most were Red Spaniards who had fled across the Pyrenees after the Republican defeat at the hands of Franco and his German and Italian allies; some were foreign comrades, veterans of the International and Abraham Lincoln Brigades. Many had done time in Sachsenhausen. They all gave off the rotten-straw smell of the barracks at Le Vernet and Gurs, where the government of the birthplace of *Liberté, Egalité, Fraternité* had seen fit to detain them as enemies of the State. With the fall of France and the replacement of *Liberté, Egalité, Fraternité* with *Travail, Famille, Patrie*, most of these *indésirables* were added to the massive slave labour pool of the *Reich*. As the last prisoner crossed the gangway, LeBlanc saluted the German naval officer smartly and got into his car. The men were driven into the foul-smelling hold, where they huddled on crude benches clearly added as an afterthought; this tub must have been a commandeered fishing boat. A bucket stood in the corner. The motor rumbled, the ship lurched more violently, and they were off. Soon a few men were taking turns retching painfully into the bucket; they had not eaten enough in months to vomit.

Peter, a Polish Communist from the Dombrowski Brigade who spoke broken Spanish and English, sat on a bench as far away as possible from the bucket. He surveyed the group, illuminated by a naked bulb. Most were similarly seated on benches, wrapped in filthy blankets, trying to roll with the ship. Perhaps they would get used to the motion enough to allow a game of cards. Suddenly a gust of sea air cut the stench. A German soldier descended into the hold. He shouted something in German, looked around at the queasy men, and returned above decks. The German speakers quickly translated. 'We're going to some kind of work facility. We will build fortifications. Anyone who does not work, who steals, all the usual things, will be shot.'

The men received this news calmly; this wasn't new. Usually, all they could think about was food. It was only the seasickness that kept these thoughts at bay. First they tried to think of nothing. Then they found themselves thinking of refreshing things that might ease the nausea: a mint leaf, a single slice of lemon, a small piece of ice. If their minds rolled like the ship and veered in the direction of chocolate, whisky, garlic, ripe cheese, the bile would rise in their throats. Steering their minds towards the bland and the cool kept their stomachs where they belonged. No sooner had most of them mastered this than two sailors appeared with pots of bitter *ersatz* coffee and a crate of suspect bread. The men who found this revolting gave their rations to the men who did not.

The light bulb went off to mark the first of two arbitrary nights. Each comrade made himself as comfortable as possible on his share of bench to encourage a fitful sleep punctuated by dreams of ice and mint, or of nothing but flat land and blue sky. When the men awoke with the light bulb's peremptory dawn, their lice had all become acquainted. Again they were served the bitter beverage and the insult to the idea of bread, this time with some 'margarine' that must have been skimmed from the dirty oil slick in the harbour. The sailors made a show of emptying the brimming slop pail, though it had already been filled a few times over, only to topple over in the pitching hold. Most of its contents flowed aft, away from the benches, but the odour added itself to the cacophony of rotting fish, vomit and ancient dirt. Peter looked at Little Juan (one of four Juans) and smiled.

'Juancito, it is like trench warfare, only the trenches move.'

'Yes,' replied Juan, smiling with blackened teeth. '*Camarada*, I almost have nostalgia.'

CHAPTER 22

Paris, 1931

Farewell, snow, desert, rocks, eternity,
Enraged and tender mouth, necessary storms.
The loud ghost whom you said you knew,
You know his name at last and do not dare say it.
Follow with your eyes the comet about to disappear
Outside your universe, in an ignored sky.

You would roll in his train with inebriated suns
Your spirit made rebellious by your untamed body...
Remain alone and standing in your pride of copper
With the dead dreams which rot your nights,
The croaked stars, disgusting with sperms
And the flabby women, lovers forever abandoned...
But you understand too late, when the horizon closes up,

Your heart caught in the door and your hands crushed.
Fleeing the blind sky and the worried sea,
You build for yourself alone boring Paradises,
But each rising dawn confirms your defeat
And chases away the shadow seated at the foot of your
    bed.

Must one live again still, live eternally
The desperate night, the unending day,
And for a brief respite cowardly wish

To fall asleep dead drunk, with one's forehead on some
    table?

For the lying mouth and the disloyal hand,
For the powerless heart which knew not love,
For the body enslaved to uneventful pleasures
And for fleeing eyes, there is no recourse.

A shivering bird turns in the black sky.
Were the bird catcher to leave the cage open,
It will fall, with its wing beating and its heart heavy with
    hope.
The north wind is cold on the deserted plain.

But you, you who knew how to cross mirrors,
You don't even know, in the pitiful night,
How to find the house of the irrevocable master.
The infallible formula has lost its power.

Faithfully followed by the funeral entourage
Of shame, remorse and livid dreads,
You will always be searching, dragging your dead soul
Which bears upon its neck the trace of your fingers.

Claude Cahun

CHAPTER 23

La Rocquaise, St Brelade

December 1941

Thank God for the wireless. They listened to BBC and the powerfully intrusive German stations sporadically during the day; often Lucille would take notes on the nine o'clock BBC news broadcast and, with Suzanne's illustrations, turn these into missives from the Nameless Soldier. They liked to think the recent rumours of multiple desertions were due, in part, to their efforts. More Orders against the Jews had appeared, spelling out the means by which proceeds from terminated Jewish businesses were to be handled. The local government that had been Marlene's place of employment was now the agent of her persecution. They wanted to turn her in to the Nazis; they might even be looking for her actively. Her colleagues had become jerrybags and informers. The fact of a Jewish father, formerly just a curiosity, was now a dangerous secret. Lucille and Suzanne, Mary Drummond and the wireless were her new family. She had got to know the newsreaders; they now often introduced themselves before reading the report in order to prevent impostors from passing on propaganda. Alvar Liddell, Bruce Belfridge, Frederick Grisewood and Godfrey Talbot were cousins who came to her home bearing news that they wanted her to hear from their own lips. They pulled no punches, but they never went to pieces. They did not lecture or condescend like Haw-Haw, who would be more depressing if he didn't sound so pompous. Haw-Haw was the tippling uncle on German Overseas Radio whom

79

everyone made lame jokes about. Churchill, though his speech often sounded somewhat slurred, was a more beloved uncle whose faults were overlooked in the face of his unrelenting optimism and eloquence. Although Mr Orange had been an example of an untrustworthy authority figure, she couldn't bring herself to think the same about Churchill; it made her nauseous with fear. What if all of them were in on it? What if Churchill was making the 'V' sign with one hand and taking *Reichsmarks* with the other? She shivered and quickly argued the thought away before it drew tears.

With a history book with maps borrowed from Lucille and Suzanne's vast library, she began sorting out the different locations mentioned on the wireless: Tunis, Berlin, Kiev, Singapore. She wanted to put a map of the world on the wall and put pins in locations where war was being waged; she wanted to put a big pin on Jersey. Maybe she should just put a pin in her heart, to locate her on the map of suffering which unfolded almost worldwide. It became the world itself, really, and not a map. She was just a pin, a dot. She could put nothing on her heart, especially not a monogram. She could be taking her life in her hands if she wore a monogrammed sweater; the thought made her chuckle.

They sat in the living room after a Sunday dinner of bread and swedes, sipping wine. They had managed to scrounge enough wood for a small fire, so each woman needed only a single shawl to ward off the chill. They switched on the wireless at nine to listen to the news. Alvar Liddell came on and began announcing a surprise attack by Japan on a place in the Pacific belonging to the United States, Pearl Harbor. Marlene had never heard of Pearl Harbor; she looked towards Suzanne and Lucille, who were listening intently with unreadable expressions. When Liddell had finished, they looked at each other. 'This is bad for America,' said Suzanne, 'but I think it is good for Europe. I think America will join the war now; they will defeat the Germans.'

Lucille interjected. 'But *cherie*, America has always been averse to this war. They want nothing to do with our problems; they are capitalist.'

'True, Lucille, but they to some extent incited this. They cut off Japan's oil supply. Surely they knew that would lead to something.'

'I suppose. But they still have to decide to enter the war.'

'Yes. Well, time will tell.'

'This is a good opportunity, though, for that letter to the jerries we were planning: "Hitler leads us."'

Suzanne, smiling, took it up: '"Goebbels speaks for us. Goering eats for us."'

'"Himmler … Himmler murders for us."'

'But nobody dies for us!'

CHAPTER 24

Paris

1933

Though he emerged better educated, Peter's prison record in Poland stripped him of the few rights he otherwise would have had. In late 1933 he set out for Paris with a false passport and the Party's blessing. He immediately found a Party cell and a job. Though he worked illegally, the Party was legal in France and he was astonished by the casual air of the meetings, with no look-out posted to watch for the police. *L'Humanité*, the French Communist newspaper, was sold everywhere. So was the fascist paper, *Action Française*.

The threat of fascism was palpable; shortly after his arrival, Peter almost lost his life outside the *Palais Bourbon*, countering anti-Semitic right-wing rioters protesting an alleged Jewish/government conspiracy that ended in the mysterious death of one Serge Stavisky.

Peter continued working with the Polish Communists, selling the Yiddish-language *Naje Presse* and the Polish *Dziennik Ludowy* (Daily Worker), doing the odd job. Then Madrid was bombed in 1936; the Spanish Civil War had begun. This became the sole topic of conversation among both Communists and Social Democrats, who had put aside their enmity and formed the *Front Populaire* to respond to the immediacy of the fascist onslaught. People began to make their way to Spain to join the rapidly-forming International Brigades. The town of Albacete was their staging area. Peter joined the Jaroslaw Dombrowski battalion of Poles (named after a Polish member of the Paris commune) in the XIIth brigade, fighting side-by-side with Anarchists, Socialists, and ordinary Poles. Many of the fighters were Jews who saw that the first half of the century was not turning in their favour; they printed their own Yiddish newspaper behind the lines. With guns and grenades and the help of the populace, they defended Madrid on the bloody Jarama Front, losing half their number, then were sent to fight the Italian fascists alongside the anti-fascist Garibaldis in Guadalajara. Peter received the occasional letter from Polish comrades and his worried family; he wrote back in case his letters would actually get out: I'm fine, I'm helping the Cause, do not worry. The letters from other relatives urging him to leave Spain and go to Palestine were torn up. He was an Internationalist.

Then he began receiving news about the Great Purge; Polish Communists in the Soviet Union for one reason or another were rounded up and executed; Stalin never forgave their earlier enthusiasm for Trotsky. A year later, the Polish Communist Party was dissolved. The fascists received more reinforcements from their friends the Nazis and strove to cut the Republican defenders in two. A slow retreat began. Amid raids from the new Stuka divebombers, through burning towns, Peter and his comrades withdrew. The Dombrowski Brigade was reorganised into the XIIIth. Ever optimistic, they engaged the enemy for four months at the Ebro River.

The fascists were using Portuguese, Moroccan, Italian and German forces to great effect; the League of Nations thought a withdrawal of International Brigades would be mirrored by a withdrawal of foreigners on the other side, it being the twentieth century, and people having learned so much from the Great War. The fascists and their allies saw this as their great opportunity and pressed on, finally taking Madrid.

CHAPTER 25

The Evening Post

Sixth Order relating to measures against Jews.

February 7th 1942.

In virtue of the plenary powers conferred upon me
by the Führer and the Supreme Commander of the
Wehrmacht, I order as follows:

§ 1.
Prohibition on being out of doors.
No Jew shall be outside his residence between the
hours of eight o'clock in the evening and six
o'clock in the morning.

§ 2.
Prohibition on change of residence.
No Jew shall change his present place of
residence.

§ 3.
Penalties.
Any person who contravenes the provisions of this
Order shall be liable to imprisonment and a fine,
or to either of such penalties. In addition, the
offender may be interned in a camp for Jews.

§ 4.
Commencement.
This Order shall come into force as from the
promulgation thereof.

The Military Commander in France.

CHAPTER 26

Norderney Camp
Alderney, Channel Islands

March 1942

Most of them made it through the winter. Those who had preceded them told them they were on Alderney, a windswept and almost treeless island that had been abandoned by most of its inhabitants. They aided the completion of rows of barracks started by the better-off Belgians and Vichy French; several had died from beatings by the Germans or the camp police. Now they settled, if that was the right word, into a routine of fourteen-hour days of quarry work, which involved the endless crushing of stone. Exhaustion and filth, starvation and beatings, all punctuated by watery soup and sawdust 'bread'. Those who exchanged their 'bread' for cigarettes died more quickly. The survivors became adept at swiping the errant beetroot or cabbage leaf from the garbage, trading cigarettes with the kitchen girls for potato peelings. The Spaniards kept to themselves, as did the Poles and Belgians. The contractor they were all 'working' for, *Organisation Todt*, treated the Spaniards and Belgians a little more leniently than the Poles, who were considered sub-human. Peter was able to stay with the Spanish detail but could circulate among the Poles because of his origins; this gave him more access to camp news. Rumours of the war were rampant: it was going poorly for the Germans and would soon be over, it was going well for them, the Americans had entered, Britain was going to capitulate.

Peter hefted his hammer, brought it down wearily on a rock. Rock dust and grit powdered his hair, saturated his rags, filled his thin shoes. Every movement was painful; his muscles were sore and grit constantly abraded his skin. If he had had more energy for a sense of humour, he would have compared himself to a rasp or one of those small files used by women on their fingernails. It bothered him that he was so weakened by hunger that he couldn't swing the hammer well, his arms often failing to generate enough momentum to carry it through a swing, leaving him to jump dizzily out of the way as the thing dropped out of its arc. Why should it bother me, he wondered. It's not as if I'm working for the Revolution; I'm working for beasts who consider me a beast. The whole thing was crazy; if they really wanted work from us, why did they starve us? If they wanted to kill us, why didn't they kill us? If they pay us, why is there nothing to buy? When they were stronger, he and his comrades used to debate this. Now they mainly communicated by looks. Every look said the same thing: 'This is a living hell. How long will it last until we are free or dead?'

The Juans had made it thus far. Little Juan slowly pushed a wheelbarrow towards Peter's little pile of stones. He looked at Peter with a mixture of exhaustion and pity. Peter managed a gritty smile.

'Juancito, they are making the rocks harder today.'

'Pedro, look in my pocket.'

Peter glanced towards the guard, saw that his back was turned, looked towards Little Juan's bulging patch pocket, and reached inside. He took out a half beetroot covered in sawdust.

'*Gracias, camarada.*'

'*De nada.*'

Peter eyed the beetroot, rubbed it on his shirt, exchanging sawdust for rock grit, and devoured it.

Juan lingered, taking his time loading the rocks.

'I am helping one of the French girls. She did not want to be a whore, so they work her to death in the kitchen. She can help us get more food.'

'What do you do for her in return?'

'I give her cigarettes, I listen to her. The poor girl. I piss on the mothers of these Nazis.'

Peter brought his hammer down hard on a rock. Juan hauled his load away in the rickety wheelbarrow. Dr Todt counted his money.

CHAPTER 27

May 1942

Seventh Order relating to Measures against Jews

March 24th, 1942; registered by Act of the Royal
Court dated 9th May, 1942.

In virtue of the plenary powers conferred upon me
by the Führer and the Supreme Commander of the
Wehrmacht, I order as follows:

§ 1.
For paragraph (1) of § 1 of the Third Order of
April 26th, 1941, relating to measures against
Jews (VOBIF p. 255) there shall be substituted
the following paragraph —

(1) Any person having at least three
grand-parents of pure Jewish blood shall be
deemed to be a Jew. A grand-parent having been a
member of the Jewish religious community shall
ipso jure be deemed to be of pure Jewish blood.
Any person having two grand-parents of pure
Jewish blood who —
  (a) on June 25th, 1940, or thereafter, was a
     member of the Jewish religious community; or
  (b) on June 25th, 1940, was married to a Jew
     or, thereafter, has married a Jew;
  shall be deemed to be a Jew.

In doubtful cases, any person who has been a
member of the Jewish religious community shall be
deemed to be a Jew.

§ 2.
Subsequent declaration.
Any person who, not having previously been deemed
to be a Jew, comes within the terms of § 1 of the
Third Order of April 26th, 1941, relating to

measures against Jews (VOBIF p. 255) as amended
by § 1 of this Order, shall, before May 1st,
1942, make the declarations required by § 3 of
the Order of September 27th, 1940, relating to
measures against Jews (VOIBF p. 92) and by §§ 2
and 3 of the Second Order of October 18th, 1940,
relating to measures against Jews (VOBIF p. 112)
and shall surrender the wireless receiving sets
to which § 1 of the Order of August 13th, 1941,
concerning the confiscation of wireless receiving
sets belonging to Jews (VOIBF p. 278) relates.

§ 3.
Prohibition on the carrying-on of certain
economic activities and on the employment of Jews.

(1) On and after May 1st, 1942, the provisions of
§ 3 of the Third Order of April 26th, 1941,
relating to measures against Jews (VOIBF p. 255)
which prohibit the carrying-on of certain
economic activities and the employment of Jews,
shall apply to every person who, not having
previously been deemed to be a Jew, is deemed to
be such by virtue of this Order.

(2) The like provision shall apply to
undertakings which, under this Order, are deemed
to be Jewish and for which a managing
administrator has not been appointed.

§ 4.
Employees who, by virtue of this Order, are
deemed to be Jews and who are dismissed from
their employment, shall not be entitled to claim
compensation for dismissal without due notice,
notwithstanding that it is not prohibited to
continue employing such persons.

§ 5.
This Order shall come into force as from the
promulgation thereof.

The Military Commander in France.

***

Eighth Order concerning measures against the Jews

In virtue of the plenary powers conferred upon me
by the Führer and the Supreme Commander of the
Wehrmacht, I order as follows:

§ 1
Jewish insignia.

(1) Jews from the age of six years and up are
ordered not to appear in public unless they are
wearing the Jewish star.

(2) The Jewish star is a six-pointed star the
size of the palm of the hand, outlined in black,
with a yellow ground and in black letters the
word, 'Jew.' It is to be worn visibly on the left
side of the chest, securely sewn to the clothing.

§ 2
Penalties for infractions.

Infractions of this rule are punishable by
imprisonment and fine, or by either of such
penalties. In addition or in lieu of these
penalties, the police may take the measure of
imprisoning the offender in a camp for Jews.

§ 3
Registration.

This Order was registered on 7 June, 1942.

The Military Commander in France.

==

15. June 42

Visited Dr. Casper [civilian official of the
Field Commandant office] with A.G.

We advised that this Order should not be
registered or put into execution.

91

Dr. Casper agreed. I should like no further
action at present.

A. Coutanche [Bailiff]

==

Official Journal No. 63

[Translation]

The Eighth Order concerning measures against Jews
is to be registered and the individuals notified
individually. The Order is not to be published as
it concerns only a few persons.

The Field Commandant,
Knackfuss, Col.

CHAPTER 28

St Brelade, Jersey

June 1942

America had joined the war, but it was not over. The Americans seemed preoccupied with battles in Asia; when would they strike a blow against the Nazis? The occupiers were clearly more nervous; all the wireless sets were confiscated; you could go to prison if they found you with one. Suzanne, Lucille and Marlene hid one in the ottoman in Lucille's bedroom and one in the barn. The BBC had previously broadcast instructions on the making of crystal radio sets; they had managed to make a couple and now used these principally, listening through earphones to be as inconspicuous as possible.

At night there were flyovers by the RAF; they were often awakened by bombs in the harbour or by anti-aircraft fire. The first few terrified them. Later, they would take advantage of the time awake, reach for their radios and listen to the midnight news. Often, the next morning, dew-softened leaflets were scattered on the ground. Usually they were in French. Marlene would make sure one stuck to her boot to take in; nobody wanted to pick one up and risk being seen by a neighbour with some old score to settle.

Marlene kept busy with the garden; they had a little fresh lettuce to sell. They traded radishes and eggs for wine and the occasional cheese. The poor chicken was becoming scrawny, though they treated her like royalty for the eggs she gave them. They were all losing weight. Their skin was rough and dry and their clothes stiff from the homemade soap. There was a rumour that some Austrian Jewish women from Guernsey had been deported to Poland; no good news came from there. People talked about camps, gas, death. On the BBC, Churchill had tried to sound optimistic in May ('Hitler forgot about this Russian winter … '), but the latest news was about the fall of Singapore to the Japanese. Marlene tried not to think about these things. She generally lay low, but did go into town to buy what few goods were available. When she did not have anything to do the enormity of the situation would prey on her mind, and if she did not shake her head and busy herself with something, she would soon be in tears. She knew she was not alone. Once she saw Suzanne sitting alone in the pantry, her hand over her eyes, weeping softly. This made her feel awkward, and she pretended not to notice. Sometimes at night, after the news broadcast, they would try to play charades, but Suzanne and Lucille always won because they knew so many obscure plays and films. Marlene was able to hold her own at cards.

There were labour camps on Jersey, run by the foreign and local employees of *Organisation Todt*. The women sometimes saw prison trucks racing from one worksite to another, filled with gaunt, filthy men. The residents who lived closer to the camps told horrifying stories of men being beaten and left to die at the worksites themselves, or on the side of the road. Many escaped; some were hidden; others turned in to curry favour with the jerries. At the *Lager* Himmelman near St Ouen's, *OT* men supervised the building of a railway by starving slave workers. The three women often gave radishes and beetroot to friends who made a point of leaving them for the prisoners as they were marched to a work detail.

The summer passed. Instead of sunning and bathing, residents tiptoed over the mined beaches scrounging for shellfish to supplement their diets while the Germans looked the other way. The moans of thirsty, starving men in the labour camps were heard in St Ouen's; the railroad extended on a bed of crushed stones, bones and blood.

CHAPTER 29

8 July 1942

Ninth Order concerning measures against the Jews

In virtue of the plenary powers conferred upon me by the Führer and the Supreme Commander of the Wehrmacht, I order as follows:

§ 1
Prohibition against the frequenting of places of entertainment and other public venues.

It is prohibited for Jews to frequent places of entertainment and other public venues in general.
   Special restrictions will be designated by the SS and Chief of Police.

§ 2
Restrictions on visits to commercial establishments.

Jews may not enter department stores, retail stores, and artisans' shops to do their shopping or to shop for others except between the hours of 3 and 4 p.m.

§ 3
Exceptions.

Specially designated Jewish enterprises are excepted from the prohibitions delineated in paragraphs 1 and 2.

§ 4
Penalties for infraction.

Infractions of this rule are punishable by imprisonment and fine, or by either of such penalties.

§ 5
Police measures.

In addition or in lieu of these penalties, the police may take the measure of imprisoning the offender in a camp for Jews.

§ 6
Time this measure goes into effect.

This measure goes into effect on the day of its publication.

The Military Commander in France.

CHAPTER 30

English Channel

July 1942

Several men died in the boat, including one of the two remaining Juans. They figured out that they were going south, not east to Cherbourg. Unlike their voyage to Alderney, there was no food provided at all, only water sloshed onto the deck, to be caught with cupped hands or any handy container. The slop bucket emptied itself whenever they hit rough seas. The voyage took one day and one night because of bad weather. Peter had dysentery; he had no appetite but was desperately thirsty and feverish. He sat on a splintery board in the hold, wrapped in a stiff concrete sack, trying to keep the streaming filth off his feet. Juancito had found a rusty can; he used this to collect rainwater that leaked through the ceiling. He lurched over to Peter when the ship began to heave. Peter was huddled on the board, shaking, trying not to vomit or soil himself.

'*Camarada*,' whispered Juancito, 'here is some water. I can get more.'

He raised the can to Peter's lips; Peter was able to drink most of it before the ship rolled and he had to pin himself against the bulkhead. Juancito took a rag from his pocket, moistened it, and wiped Peter's forehead.

'*Gracias*, Juancito. Save the water for yourself, man. I am going to die.'

'No, no, you will not die. The fucking Germans want you to die. You will spite them.'

'You think so, eh?'

'Yes, I do. You and I, *camarada*, we have the steel *cojones*. We will get our revenge on them. Someday they will be drowning in their own shit, just as we are now.'

'And their mothers, too?'

'*Si*, and their mothers, may they burn in hell.'

Juancito brought more cans of water. One of the stronger prisoners was able to kill a rat; several of the men shared bites of the raw meat. Peter fell asleep.

He awoke from dreams of the forest to find himself still in the stinking hold. The motor was silent. He felt extremely weak, but his fever appeared to have broken. He slowly stood up and walked unsteadily to the slop pail. He was able to urinate a little; when he sat down, nothing happened. Out of habit he rose as quickly as he could to avoid the slop pail's contents if they spilled with the ship's motion, but the ship seemed not to be moving. It was very cold. He could see other prisoners sleeping on makeshift pallets and benches.

Suddenly a soldier came down from above decks and started screaming "*Raus! 'Raus!*", hitting several men with the butt of his pistol. They all stood up as well as they could and lined up at the foot of the stairs. They were marched up and off the ship, which had moored in a port. Everyone looked around; they could see buildings and people in the faint early light. They breathed lungfuls of air – air so fresh they could have wept for joy. The men were herded into two trucks that set off for whatever their next hell was slated to be. Peter and Juan managed to be in the same truck. As the truck slowed at intersections in what appeared to be a country road, a young girl or boy, sometimes an older farmer, would toss something into the truck, or hand it to whoever was on the outside. They received two apples, a few swedes and a lump of cheese this way. The spoils were not shared equally, but Peter got a small bite of cheese and a tiny piece of apple. It almost hurt to eat them. Though he had never had much use for God, he suddenly felt that God had seen him and had sent this food to alleviate his misery for an instant. He did not know whether to feel thankful or to curse this preoccupied God who only noticed him momentarily, pausing long enough to give him what might just be serving to prolong his agony. What about all the other instants? What about the beatings, the screams, the torture, the filth, the dead everywhere? Doesn't God know about them? Tears rolled down his cheeks. Please, God, don't forget us. Please please please don't don't don't. The truck screeched to a halt and they were herded off.

CHAPTER 31

```
Field Command 515

[Translation]

10th August 1942

The Bailiff of Jersey.

Official Journal No. 69 dated 15th July 1942.

The Ninth Order concerning measures against Jews
dated 8th July 1942 is to be registered. The Jews
are to be notified of the contents in writing.

For the Field Commandant,
Dr. Casper, O.K.V.R.


=================================================


C.R.O. [Clifford R. Orange]

Will you please notify all Jews of the content of
the Order in question. I enclose 12 copies of it
herewith and I suggest that a copy be handed to
each person affected.

Ch. D. A. [Charles Duret Aubin]
A.G. 18.8.42.
```

Clifford Orange pulled himself up to his full height (he didn't cut as imposing a figure as usual due to his thinness) and knocked on the door of the Davidson flat. The Davidsons had moved from their old place in Stopford Road to cheaper digs in Oxford Road. A small, thin woman in a faded apron with a scarf tied around her head answered.

'Yes?' she said, looking at him disdainfully.

'Madam, good day. Are you Mrs Davidson?'

'Yes, I am.'

'I am Mr Orange, the Aliens Officer. Is your husband in?'

She looked momentarily distressed, then nodded. 'Yes, he is. What do you need with him? He already closed his business.'

'Yes, I know. There is a new Order I need to give to him.'

'An Order?' She was beginning to look hostile.

'May I come in?'

'Very well.'

He entered the dark flat. It smelled, like most flats these days, of boiled swedes and damp. Mr Davidson sat in a worn chair in the parlour, looking straight ahead. Buckets sat on the floor near the door next to a heap of dirty clothes. A pile of firewood lay in the middle of the floor, too precious to keep outside. Mr Orange approached the man.

'Mr Davidson?'

The old man did not look at him. The woman had returned to the kitchen, leaving Mr Orange alone to talk to her husband.

'Sir?' Orange whispered.

The man slowly turned his head to face him. 'Are you from the vicar?' he asked, expressionless.

'No, sir, I am the Chief Aliens Officer for Jersey.'

'What do you want?'

'I have to present you with the Ninth Order.'

'The what?'

'The Ninth Order relating to measures against the Jews.'

'I'm not a Jew. I used to be Church of England.' He said this to the air, no longer looking at Mr Orange.

'Ah, but you registered as a Jew in 1940 when the Occupation began.'

'Oh. Well, I didn't, but somebody paid someone to do it. Someone is always paying someone to do things against me. I think it's the Church.'

Orange was exasperated. How could he explain everything to Davidson when he was babbling like this? He might just have to talk to Mrs Davidson again.

'Mr Davidson, this Order compels you to stay out of public places, shops, and the like. The only time you are allowed in a shop is between three and four o'clock.'

'Well, you need money to go in shops, and we haven't any.'

'I see. Actually your wife, because she's a non-Jew (on his way out to the car, he would realise that in fact she *was* a Jew, but he was loath to confront them again), may shop whenever she pleases, but you, as a registered Jew, come under the prohibitions in this Order.'

Mrs Davidson came into the parlour. She looked with contempt at Orange. 'What are you bothering him for? Can't you see he's not in his right mind? He's not even Jewish.'

'Mrs Davidson, your husband registered as a Jew in 1940. He comes under the – '

'What bloody thing is it now?' she asked, bursting into tears. Her emaciation made her complete confusion and distress all the more wretched. 'What do they want with him now? Are you going to send him away? You already got rid of his shop. We don't have hardly any money left. What do you want now?'

'Madam, I am sorry. I am simply – '

'You're bloody sorry, are you!' She began to sob and scream in an ugly choked voice. 'What kind of officer are you, taking our livelihood away? Now he's sick. He doesn't know anything any more. He talks about the Church stealing from him. It's the bloody Aliens Office! Why are you doing this to us?'

Orange sat down without knowing why. He really wanted to leave immediately, but he had to carry out the serving of the Order. Why couldn't these people cooperate? They weren't the first family to give him trouble.

'Madam, it is simply an Order from the Military Command in France. As a Jew, your husband is now forbidden to enter public buildings, theatres, and the like. He may only shop between three and four o'clock. Here is the Order.'

He proffered the piece of paper to Mrs Davidson as Mr Davidson stared into space.

'I don't want your bloody paper. It's from the bloody jerries, isn't it?'

'Yes, madam, it is.'

'Why are you telling me all this? Do you want me to go mad, too? My husband, who isn't a Jew in the first place, can't go out of the house? Are you a jerry, too?'

'No, madam, uh ... '

Suddenly Mr Davidson began to twitch; his face reddened. He stood up and glared down wildly at Orange and began to roar, 'GET OUT, YOU BLOODY THIEF! GET OUT!!! STOP STEALING! STOP WATCHING ME!!!' He flailed his arms in quick flying movements that terrified Orange. The wife was still standing there, crying and wringing her hands.

Orange stood up slowly, as if he were just finishing his tea, but his hands were trembling.

'I'm sorry to have bothered you. I need to leave this paper with you.' He tried to make himself heard above Mr Davidson's roaring and Mrs Davidson's weeping. Mrs Davidson turned to her husband, caught his hands, and started to help him back down into the chair. Orange clumsily laid the paper down on a scarred side table and tried to take his leave as quietly as possible. Mrs Davidson levelled a look of pure hatred upon him; he felt it burning through the back of his head after he had closed the door behind him. He hoped Aubin would not give him any trouble over this one; he had done his best.

He started the coughing motor and headed the car east to St Saviour. It was a hot day and he was thirsty. Why wouldn't people understand that these registrations had been ordered by the Germans, that an order was an order? He wanted to avoid repercussions at all costs. If a few people had to be inconvenienced to protect the many, so be it. Nobody had forced them to register, in any case. Now all the nasty work fell to him.

Mrs Richardson lived on Dicq Road. She was a problem case. She hadn't registered in 1940 as a Jew, but had registered as a non-Jewish citizen in 1941 when printed identity cards were ordered for the entire population. She had claimed 'N. Amsterdam, British Guiana' as her birthplace and listed her maiden name as 'Algernon'. Sometimes she listed herself as 'Erica' and sometimes as 'Mary Erica'. Aubin had asked him to investigate; the Germans suspected she was a Jew. She lived with her husband Edmund, a retired sea captain. Orange drove the short distance, passing people riding bicycles in the required single-file, nodding to officers in their cars. People trudged along the pavements, avoiding the intrusive glare of the *Feldpolizei*, who made every conversation their business.

Orange got out of the car in front of the Richardson flat carrying his envelope, went down the few stairs leading to the entrance, and knocked on the door. A moment later it was answered by a short, greying woman with a thick accent and a large nose. Dutch, he thought. A Dutch Jewess. She was wearing a steel-blue dress and little gold earrings.

'Yes, sir,' she said, looking at him a bit warily. 'Can I help you?'

'I am here to see Mrs Richardson. I am Mr Orange, the Chief Aliens Officer for Jersey.'

'I am Mrs Richardson. Will you come in, Mr Orange?'

Well, this was more like it. Just a friendly chat, citizen to citizen, he thought, looking around the well-appointed flat. Portraits and seascapes hung on the walls; a worn but beautiful Persian carpet covered the floor. The furniture looked sturdy and comfortable.

'Would you like some tea, sir?'

He wondered if it would be real tea. That would be quite good after his exhausting morning. 'Yes, Mrs Richardson, that would be very nice.'

'There isn't much real tea left. I can only make it weak.'

'That is quite all right, Mrs Richardson.'

She bustled about the hearth, stirring up the fire. The gas had been shut off again. Soon, she reappeared with a Delft teapot and cups, and some potato bread.

'I'm sorry, there's no sugar. There is a little milk, though.'

'That is all right, madam. I will take it without milk or sugar.' The weak tea helped the potato bread go down.

'Mrs Richardson,' he began, picking up the envelope and removing the Order.

'Yes, sir?'

He looked up; her words suddenly sounded choked. Indeed, her face was drained of colour as she busied herself with the teapot. Her cup rattled in its saucer; her hands must have been trembling. What an unpleasant job this was!

'I must give you the latest Order concerning Measures against the Jews.'

'But, Mr Orange, I am not Jewish.'

'Madam, I am sorry, but the Attorney General has reason to believe that you are.'

She took a long sip of tea. 'No, sir, I am not a Jewess. Unfortunately, my husband, he is ill at the moment. Otherwise he could talk to you.'

'This does not concern him, madam. It only concerns you.'

She put down her cup and saucer a little too firmly and looked at him. 'Mr Orange, please, I do not know what you are talking about.'

'Mrs Richardson, allow me to show you the Order. It is up to you whether you follow it or not.'

He held the paper in front of her. She read it slowly, her face turning paler.

'All right, Mr Orange, I have read it,' she said, looking away from him. He was pretty sure now that she was, in fact, Jewish.

'Thank you, Mrs Richardson. I trust you understand its contents.'

'Yes.'

Feeling a little uncomfortable, he finished his tea. He could not manage more than half the bread. 'I wish you a good day, Mrs Richardson.'

'Good day, Mr Orange.'

Was that a hint of a sneer in her voice? He chose to ignore it. She escorted him out. He unlocked the car, started it up, and continued on his task.

Mrs Richardson sat back on the sofa and clenched and unclenched her fists. '*Scheiss*,' she muttered, '*scheiss, scheiss, scheiss, scheiss.*' Then she did what she usually did when life had dealt her a blow. She phoned her masseur.

CHAPTER 32

St Brelade, Jersey

September 1942

In September, new terror. Unbeknownst to the Islanders, it was to pay for the British/Soviet takeover of the German embassy in Teheran. What has Teheran got to do with the Channel Islands? Both have palm trees and both were places of interest to Hitler. The Channel Islands, for defensive purposes. Iran, for its oil. Iran started out the Forties as a neutral country, but one which had often been under British and Russian/Soviet sway. Unable to attract the interest of the Americans, the Shah then approached the Third *Reich*, receiving a warm response. Several hundred German 'advisors' were stationed there, looking out for Germany's interests. As it became increasingly clear that Hitler considered Czechoslovakia to be an appetiser, Britain and the Soviet Union decided to invade and occupy Iran to protect the oil. In August 1941, they invaded and easily defeated the Iranian armed forces. British troops surrounded the German embassy in Teheran.

So one of Hitler's insane *quids pro quo* began. He wanted a number of Channel Islanders, tenfold the number of interned Germans, rounded up and sent to the Pripet Marshes on the Eastern Front. As there was ongoing fighting there, this was not practical. The *Wehrmacht* delayed successfully for a year (a popular way of dealing with impossible orders by the *Führer*; tragically, the Final Solution somehow did not seem so daunting); then, when Hitler found out nothing had happened, he turned up the heat. Now the problem was the security of the

Germans on the Channel Islands amongst so many British citizens. The Iran Germans had served their purpose and were forgotten. This time, the *Wehrmacht* sprung into action.

New photo identity cards were to be issued; there were rumours of upcoming deportations. The three women sat in the parlour, trying to decide on a plan. Marlene was rigid with fear.

'What if she and I use the same card?' asked Lucille, wringing her hands. 'I have enough disguises, so they will easily confuse us, one for the other.'

'I don't know, *cherie*,' sighed Suzanne, exhaling cigarette smoke. 'It may just bring trouble for two instead of one.'

'I should just leave, then. I am bringing trouble on you both, when you have been so good to me,' said Marlene.

'NO! We will not hear of it!' said Lucille, almost shouting. 'You are helping us as well, and you are helping the Resistance.' Suzanne nodded in agreement.

Marlene was beginning to be able to unfreeze her mind and formulate a plan, astonishing herself.

'I think we may need to hide. I don't know if anyone knows you are Jewish, but people in St Helier know my father was a Jew, and I am worried they will arrest us all.'

'People do not know we are Jews, I think,' said Lucille. 'It would be suspicious for us to disappear. Besides, we are older. They may not harm us if we are quiet.'

'Do you think so, *cherie*?' asked Suzanne. 'I do not trust the bloody jerries at all.'

'I think so, Suzanne. Anyway, do you want to live in a chicken coop?' They all laughed nervously.

'Marlene, what do you think? Do you think you should move into the cellar?'

Suzanne asked this, looking intently at Marlene. Marlene held her head in her hands.

'Yes, I think so. I am afraid. I cannot get papers. I do not want to be arrested for not having papers. I don't want to bring trouble to you …'

Lucille cut Marlene off. 'Marlene, you shall move into the cellar, but you can go out sometimes with my card. I will disguise you.' She glanced at Suzanne, who looked a little less doubtful than she had a moment before.

'Is that all right with you, dear Marlene?'

'Yes, yes. It's all right.'

'Very well, then. Let us set up the cellar.'

A camp bed was placed on the cool stone floor; it could be hidden easily in an emergency. One of the wireless sets was put in a cloth bag buried under the sand in a box used to hold carrots, swedes and potatoes over the winter. Marlene hung her coat on a nail at the back door upstairs in case she needed to leave in a hurry. She was given brown and red wigs to keep with her.

The next day, Suzanne and Lucille went to register. Lucille was right; the officials did not know they were Jews, or did not let on if they did. When they were required to post a list of the house's residents inside the front door, only two names were listed. Marlene had again disappeared.

The rumours proved accurate; all English-born non-permanent residents were to be deported to internment camps, one step up from concentration camps in that they could receive Red Cross parcels, in Germany. This was announced on 15 September; the deportations began the next day.

All over the islands, the parish constables served evacuation notices to people who didn't know Teheran from Stratford-on-Avon. The hurried packing of suitcases ensued.

Some people 'disappeared'; one committed suicide. Mr Davidson, all his fears realised (except for the primacy of the Church's role), was judged insane and hospitalised. The other Jews, banned from public places and without income, treated by their government in a way which would later be called Kafkaesque, sick with apprehension, trembled inside their homes and hiding places.

Suzanne and Lucille wrote a new letter on gummed paper and pasted it on Nazi police car windows:

The cowardly police bureaucrats, who live on lies and shameful cruelty, will be DESTROYED by the Soldiers Without Names.

CHAPTER 33

Lager Himmelman, Jersey

October 1942

Peter had been put in with the Ukrainians and other *Untermenschen* slated to be worked to death. Juancito and the other Spaniards received poor treatment, to be sure, but a little more food and even some money. This, Juancito tried to share with Peter.

The five a.m. banging on the ceiling rail heralded a new day of suffering. Everyone sprang as quickly as he could from his bunk; the slowest were beaten. They filed out to the mess line, where brown lukewarm water was doled out by a sneering *OT* worker. After the thirty seconds or so allotted to drinking this breakfast, a whistle sounded and they lurched to attention. Roll was called; a few more men were beaten. Then they were marched out of the camp and onto the road; this time they were not being trucked to the worksite. Peter and Juancito, coming from their separate barracks, managed to wind up next to each other as usual. Juancito looked especially ashen.

'What's the matter, *camarada*?' asked Peter, when he thought he could risk a whisper. Both men noticed they were being marched on a different route onto the one used to take them to the railroad site.

'I think I am going to die.'

'Why? Are you sick?'

'No, no more than you. I just saw something last night in my barracks that makes me want to die.'

'What?'

'Someone had been caught stealing cabbage. We had a different head guard; I never saw him before. He hated Spaniards; I think he had been in the Condor Legion in the Spanish War, and he just hated everything about Spain. He pulled the man to the middle of the barracks and then called for one of the man's friends. His friend stood up; he was ordered to kill the man.'

'Oh, God.' Could it get any worse? 'What did he do?'

'The man begged his friend to kill him, to save the others. They were both crying. His friend tried to raise his hand against him, but could not. The filthy Nazi bastard hit both of them, then called up another friend, from the same village in Andalusia, to kill the man. Everyone was sick. Some men were crying and praying. The second friend started kicking the man, screaming and crying and laughing. It took for ever, Pedro, for ever. The man was awake for most of it. Finally, he died. Oh, God! Where was Your mercy? The Nazi left. The second friend hanged himself during the night. They left his body in the barracks when they marched us out.'

Juancito was choking with sobs as he marched.

'Oh, Pedro, what will we do? What if they want me to kill you, or you to kill me? Oh, shit, I cannot do this any more!'

He fell to his knees. Peter quickly grabbed him and held him up.

'Stay up, Juancito. Please, I don't know what to do. We are in different barracks. It won't happen.'

'No, no, it can happen anywhere! I don't want to kill you! I don't want you to kill me!' He was wailing; it was starting to draw the attention of a guard.

'We will think of something, *camarada*, don't worry. Maybe we can agree on something in case it happens.'

'What can we agree on? This is insane!'

Juancito had managed to stop crying; he now looked angry. Peter noted with self-disgust that he felt even more fearful.

Juancito continued. 'What if one kills the other, and then kills himself? Then it's only two people involved instead of three.'

'I am not going to kill you like a rat. Rats kill their young, not humans.'

'You have my permission, *camarada*. If it comes to that, I want you to kill me. You don't even have to kill yourself afterwards; you know I gave you permission. Holy Mother of God, why are we in hell? Why have you forgotten us?' Now he was crying again.

'It's not the Mother of God, it's the fucking fascists. Remember that.'

Peter did not dare ask Juan what he wanted if he, Peter, was chosen for death; Juan was in no condition to talk about it, needing all his strength to march. They trudged on in silence, on an unfamiliar road. They approached a hill. As they got closer, they could see holes in the rocky sides. They were herded with truncheons into one hole, which turned out to be a tunnel. They were handed picks and shovels and driven deep into the damp interior of several tunnels, which they were called upon to excavate further. A few men were given trolley carts to remove the debris. The rumble of what turned out to be a cement mixer was heard far off. They were building a hospital, of all things. The tiny bit of mercy these swine had was spent on their bloodthirsty fellows-in-arms, to get them back to battle as quickly as possible. The dead of the *Untermenschen* would be the foundation of the hospital. What do you call such a place, Peter wondered bitterly, his mouth trembling. The Charnel House Hospital? The Murderers' Polyclinic? He shakily raised his pick and began to chip away at the rock. It truly felt like digging his own grave.

CHAPTER 34

St Helier, Jersey

August 1942

Albert Bedane, born in France, naturalised British subject, ladies' man and masseur extraordinaire, held his physiotherapy clinic in one of the properties he had acquired through marriage to his wealthy and uncomplaining wife Clara. It was called Greenwood, on Roseville Street. Mrs Richardson was only one of his myriad clients. There was nothing out of the ordinary about her calling him.

'Hello, Bedane here.'

'Albert? It's Mrs Richardson.'

'Mrs Richardson, how are you?' He pictured her in his mind instantly; a tiny pleasant older woman with a Dutch accent, often with painful knees; always paid her bill promptly.

'I, uh, well, I am fine, but I need a massage.'

'Oh, are your knees bothering you, dear?'

'Yes, that's right.'

'I have an opening at two p.m.. Can you stop over then?'

'Yes, thank you.'

Her knees really weren't so badly off; her neck muscles, though, were tight as bowstrings. She had waved off the usual chaperoning by his nurse (a ladies' man needs to take precautions, but with someone Mrs Richardson's age it didn't look very suspicious not to have another lady present). He worked on her neck as she gasped.

'Mrs Richardson, your neck is awfully tight today, I must say. Did you not sleep well?'

'No, Albert, I slept well. I did have a fright, though.'

'What happened?'

'Promise you won't tell anyone.'

'You know I won't.'

'Yes, I know. Well, someone from the Aliens Office came by with a paper saying that Jews cannot go out in public except between three and four o'clock.'

'Three and four o'clock?' He dug his knuckles into her trapezius muscles, willing them to yield. 'That's dreadful! Why did they bring it to you?'

'They think I'm Jewish.'

'Oh, dear.'

'I mean, maybe my *zayd* – uh, I mean my grandfather might have been, but I always consider myself to be Dutch only. I didn't register back when the occupation began and they made the Jews register.'

'I see.' He made her turn onto her back; he moved her head back and forth as if she were saying 'no'.

'Albert, do you think they will deport the Jews? Even now, they cannot work. They are locked in their houses.'

'I don't know, dear, but I don't think it's out of the question. One hears terrible things coming out of Poland.' He dug into her sternocleidomastoids; she remained tensed up.

'Yes. I know. I don't know what to do. I don't want to be locked in my house. I don't want to be deported. Someone has to help Edmund. He's having more trouble getting around, you know.'

'No, I didn't know that. I'd suggest you bring him round here for a massage, but I know what a stubborn old bird he is.'

'Yes, my Edmund is stubborn. Perhaps he shall outlive us all.' She tensed up more, undoing Albert's work. 'At the rate things are going, it might be easy to outlive me.'

'Oh, dear, don't say such things!' He stopped massaging and looked at her. Now his eyes were welling up.

'I don't know what to do, Albert! What if they take me away?'

He sat her up and looked into her eyes. 'Mrs Richardson, look at me. I don't want you to worry like this. I don't know what is going on these days. The world is so crazy. The jerries are pigs.' This he said in a whisper. 'Look, I might be able to help you. Right now, I need you to relax so that you do not make yourself ill. I don't think anything is going to happen right now. If something does happen, come straight over here, all right?'

'Thank you, Albert! You are very kind!'

'Not at all, Mrs Richardson. Now go home and give my regards to your husband.'

'Thank you!'

She didn't skip down the pavement exactly, but her step was lighter and her neck a little looser. Bedane saw another client, then quietly went down the cellar stairs. He stooped to look around with an electric torch; the ceiling was low, but not too low for someone short.

CHAPTER 35

St Brelade, Jersey

Autumn 1942

During the day Marlene had a light in the cellar, and could take quick trips to the bathroom upstairs. At night, it had to be completely dark. At dusk, if she had ventured upstairs, she would sadly make her way down the stairs with a hard-boiled egg or some bread and cut-up swede and a flask of water, to sit in darkness. She became expert in listening to the footsteps on her ceiling. She could distinguish Suzanne's slow tread from Lucille's brisker one. She could hear their muffled voices and those of visitors. Usually, sleep would come early in the evening because of the boredom of sitting or lying in the dark on her camp bed, though she tried to keep awake in order to catch the BBC broadcast at nine. Eventually, she arranged with Lucille and Suzanne for one of them to stamp her foot on the floor a little before nine to wake her for the broadcast. She would slip the earphone in, attach one wire to the nearby water pipe with a tiny clip, and manipulate the cat's whisker on the little crystal until the voice came in. As before, when planes kept her awake she would listen to the midnight broadcast. She often found herself waking up in the morning with the earphone in place.

There was seldom a mention of the Channel Islands' plight; the BBC probably did not want to antagonise the Nazi occupiers. She did not understand many of the things they reported; she still did not know where half the places they mentioned were. When the announcer sounded upbeat and optimistic, that was good enough for her. She was happy to hear another human voice in the darkness, one that spoke the King's English, one without a barely concealed undertone of panic. It was easy to believe that these announcers knew of her existence. After all, they were also talking to Londoners sitting in bomb shelters and cellars. She kept wondering which was worse, being bombed or occupied. It was like comparing a quick death with a slow one.

Somewhere in England a late-twentysomething woman like herself was lying in a cellar or a bomb shelter, thinking the same thing. Listening to Charles Gardner, Marlene wondered if she would ever lie in bed with a man and listen to him talk to her. She hugged her lumpy pillow. Lucille and Suzanne had each other; no matter how scared they were, they could talk to each other in bed, make each other chuckle, hug and kiss. Marlene had nobody but the BBC to keep her company in the long awful nights. She shed some tears, but soon stopped. It wouldn't do any good. If she fell apart, she was doomed. After the broadcast she removed the sandy earphone, put the set away, and flung herself down to sleep.

But she couldn't. She had probably been dozing early in the evening with the darkness coming sooner. She lay on the camp bed, covering herself with the thin woollen blanket.

A tiny scritch-scratching in the corner signalled the presence of a mouse. This would keep her awake for some time; she hated mice, even though she knew she had much worse things to fear. Mice probably had it as good as they ever had; they could find just as much food as before the war. Now humans were living more like rodents, hiding in cellars, eating bits of thrown-away food, scurrying into the darkness. Perhaps one day she would tune in the BBC and hear squeaking and scratching, heralding the complete transformation of the

119

radio audience into another species. Maybe there would be a special programme for people like her, who were suddenly considered Jews. She knew little about being Jewish; her father's family had not approved of his marriage to her mother, so she had not got to know a Jewish family. She wondered if they had left in the evacuation before the Occupation, or if they had turned into mice like her. If they all made it through the war, would they want to meet her? Were there ways to learn to be Jewish? She knew about the pebble on the gravestone; she also knew they did many things with candles. She shifted on the flimsy bed; the mouse heard her and stopped scratching. She imagined the BBC Mouse Broadcast, telling listeners how to make beds from lint, how to make a meal from a single pea, and reading the poems of terrified Jewish mice who lit tiny candles in cellars while Nazi boots thundered overhead.

CHAPTER 36

La Rocquaise, St Brelade

November 1942

The chicken was dead; their days were limned by hunger. Upon awakening, weak parsnip coffee and a small quantity of milk and bread. Lunch: Surrealist swede slices and 'coffee' or wine, maybe a potato. Dinner: more of the same. Without eggs, without Marlene's help in the garden, with the necessity of keeping low profiles, Lucille and Suzanne lacked the means to put more on the table. None of their neighbours knew of the Nameless Soldier work. Mary Drummond had been caught and, when they last heard, was being sent to a women's camp called *Ravensbrück*. Marlene read the strain on their faces. She listened more intently than ever to the BBC, cheering on the British forces as they fought the Axis, listening in vain for a mention of the Channel Islands. Early in the month, The British Eighth Army had defeated the Germans at El Alamein in North Africa. Bruce Belfridge had sounded very excited on the wireless. Their spirits lifted, Lucille and Suzanne were shortly clacking away on typewriters, readying the news for the jerries in case their commanders were keeping it a secret. But where was the army to liberate Jersey and Guernsey and Alderney and Sark? Why were they never even mentioned on the wireless? She was happy for the denizens of El Alamein, somewhere in North Africa, but what about Jersey? What about all the deportees? The Channel Islands were being hidden in a cellar just as she was.

One night, she was dreaming of the past. She dreamt of her

mother's fried potatoes, like little pillows, falling open in the centre. She dreamt of garlicky fish and red wine, of yellow butter and white cream on scones, of rich vanilla ice cream. She dreamt of going to the beach in mid-morning, gingerly walking down the red granite stairs to the narrow strip of sand that widened to almost a football pitch by the late afternoon at low tide. She had had an itchy aqua wool swimming costume and an old quilt her mother had made. She would sit on the quilt, often with her friend Alice Chevalier, and read a book or watch the tourists. In cooler weather she and Alice would take their bicycles and ride west to feed the ducks in their favourite little stream in St Brelade, or watch the seabirds in the bay. On rainy days they would often sit in Marlene's flat, doing embroidery ('For my trousseau,' Alice would say with a dreamy expression) or playing draughts. Eventually, Alice did marry one of her beaus. Marlene seldom encountered her afterwards. As all her friends married, she found herself befriending the next generation of girls at her office. They were fun for a beach day or the cinema, but she found them flighty and shallow, and she suspected they felt she was a drying-up old maid. Invitations to parties became infrequent, which upset her, though she knew she had always been a fifth wheel.

She was awakened by shouting and frenzied stomping on the floor with what sounded like high heels. She began to shake. Was this the end? Were they all being arrested? Suddenly, Suzanne came tearing down the stairs.

'Marlene! Come up quickly and help us!'

Marlene leapt up and took the stairs two at a time with Suzanne in the lead. Suzanne frantically pushed her into the bathroom. Lucille was bending over the tub, covered in blood, shrieking. Like a wild animal, Marlene thought, until she saw the pig in the tub. Screaming, squirming, spraying blood, it was trying to get away from the knife-wielding Lucille.

'*Merde!* Help me do this!' she shouted above the screams. 'I don't know what to do! Marlene, grab its front legs! Suzanne! Get out of the way!'

Marlene, shaking violently, approached the tub and tried to grasp its front legs, which were slippery with blood. She finally managed to pin the legs awkwardly against the side of the tub. Lucille plunged the knife into the pig's throat. It stopped screaming, but thrashed violently with a sickening terminal energy. Towels flew, bottles of pills shattered on the floor, Suzanne vomited into the toilet. Marlene felt faint and sat on the sticky floor. The pig finally stopped moving.

'Get up, you two!' snarled Lucille. 'I don't know how to do this. We have to butcher it. I think we have to remove the intestines first.'

Suzanne straightened up. Marlene started to cry.

'Marlene, *cherie*. Please get up. We will get everything cleaned up and then we will have meat. I need you to help me.'

Marlene stood up and looked into the tub. The pig's blood was slowly going down the drain. She smelled urine and faeces; she was relieved to realise they were the animal's.

Lucille took the knife and slit open the belly. Intestines cascaded out.

'Get me a bucket.'

Suzanne ran out, returned with a bucket that was soon filled with guts.

'These I think we can bury. I don't think we'll be making sausage.'

They ran a cold shower (when had they last had hot water? They couldn't remember) to wash off the carcass. They skinned it, saving the skin. Fortunately, it was winter, so spoilage was not an immediate concern. They removed the heart, sliced it, and sautéed it with a tiny onion. It was quickly devoured.

'We are like Bacchantes,' said a recovered Suzanne. 'I do not care about the blood. I just want to fill my belly.'

'You cared about the blood in the bathroom, *cherie*.' They laughed. Then they went back into the bathroom, pulled out the liver, and sautéed it. They ate it standing over the pan. Reinvigorated, they cut up the rest of the pig, wrapped the pieces in writing paper, put them in a wooden box, and set the box outside the back door.

'The dogs will get it!'

'I don't think so.'

'No, they will! Where will we put it? We can't put it on the roof!'

'Why not?'

'It will attract too much attention.'

'No, let's do it!'

The box was dragged up the stairs, pushed through an opened window onto a flat part of the roof. They eventually ate every scrap of meat, made soup from the bones, rendered the fat, tanned the skin with lye and gave it to Marlene for a blanket.

CHAPTER 37

The Underground Hospital Site, Jersey

April 1943

The Hospital of Death grew underground. Dynamite blew holes deeper and deeper; if a few slaves died inside, there were always more to replace them. The bodies were put into the food trucks, to be taken away after 'meals'. The distinction between soldiers and *Organisation Todt* workers was blurry; either could be monstrous or indifferent. None was kind.

On the other hand, the distinction between Spaniards and other 'Aryans', and the Slavic *Untermenschen*, was usually followed. The Spaniards got some money and were even allowed out of the camp on their two Sundays per month off. They bought and began wearing ridiculous bowler hats to protect their heads from the falling debris. The *Untermenschen* grew more emaciated. Most used rags to replace their long-ago-worn-out shoes and clothes. It helped to have a Spanish friend.

Peter and Juancito lifted rocks with raw, bleeding hands into a trolley. They were quite weak, and worked slowly. They husbanded their waning strength in order to last until noontime, when they were given cards redeemable for 'soup', which was a joke, but which at least quenched their thirst. In the afternoon they did the same thing until the 'bread' and swede that were supper. Those who had not died were marched back to *Lager* Himmelman.

Juancito had not recovered from the sight he had witnessed.

His hands shook frequently, and he often looked to be on the verge of tears. He was at least able to work; Peter saw to that, trying to whisper the odd word of encouragement. This afternoon, he stacked rocks in the trolley in such a way as to fill up a great deal of space with a smaller mass of rocks and gave this to Juancito to trundle out. He was dismayed when Juancito was unable to push the fourth lightened load of the shift.

'I cannot do this shit, *camarada*. I don't know what to do.'

'Try again, Juancito.'

It was obvious Juancito was having trouble. Tears were beginning to form in his eyes.

'I'll take it. Start breaking up more rocks, and I'll be back.'

Peter handed him the hammer, which he knew he couldn't lift, and started out of the tunnel with the creaking trolley. He did not want Juancito to see his own tears. This man had been a fearless revolutionary, the scourge of the Spanish fascists; now he was being worked to death and struggling to make it through each day of anguish.

The trolley bumped over a dent in the track; at the same time he heard a muffled thud behind him, followed by screams. He turned to see that the end of the tunnel had collapsed, crushing some immediately and trapping others in the rubble. The light there had been extinguished; he could hardly see in the choking dust but ran towards the screams. He could hear Juancito screaming and crying, 'Pedro, Pedro, I cannot get out!' among the other weak and terrified calls for help. Suddenly a bright torch shone from the tunnel mouth; their shadows were cast on the dust in the tunnel; ghosts of ghosts. A loud voice ordered him and the others to halt. Two officers, one carrying a large torch, both carrying pistols, strode forward into the chaos. They ordered those not crushed by the rocks to leave the tunnel at once. One emphasised the order by striking the nearest worker on the shoulder with the butt of his weapon. Peter stood frozen; others did also, listening helplessly to the screams of the trapped men, watching the strange quivering silhouettes in the dust.

'*Mach schnell!!*' screamed one of the Germans. He aimed his gun at the man he had pistol-whipped and shot him in the head. The report of the pistol echoed endlessly, drowning out the pleadings of the trapped slaves. The officers ordered the others out of the tunnel, leaving the dead and the trapped behind.

Peter walked out on shaky legs. He had pissed himself. He was trying not to cry. The group of surviving slaves was turned over to an *Organisation Todt* worker who made them sit on the ground while he decided what to do with them. Other workers were already arriving to block up the tunnel entrance with timbers and stones. *Juancito* was dying inside. Peter sat immobile on the ground with the others. Many sobbed; others stared straight ahead, unable to feel any more, waiting with a sickening patience for the next order. The *OT* worker regarded them all with disgust.

Then it was time to go back to the *Lager*. His group brought up the rear of the column. He began to tremble all over again, but forced himself to march. They were stopped when a convoy of supply trucks crossed their path. Most of the guards went up to the head of the column to greet their comrades in the trucks; one guard remained behind. They were on an unpaved road with trees lining each side. Some part of Peter's mind was working, thinking of escape. It worked above his anguish and grief, worked away like a pocket watch in his shirt. This part of his mind ticked away as he eyed a filthy piece of canvas, probably an old truck cover, muddied with tyre tracks, on the opposite side of the road.

Suddenly, the remaining guard in the rear ran halfway up the column of about two hundred to kick a man who had fainted. Peter drifted back to the end of the column. As they began their slow march he stopped walking and then dropped to his knees and crawled to the side of the road where the canvas was, flattening himself out on the ground and pulling the cloth over himself. Some prisoners saw what he was doing, but the guard had not returned. The men trudged on. The dust and soot in the canvas and on the road mixed with Peter's sweat, urine, and tears to form a sparse mud, the purest distillation of agony. Racked with exhaustion and pain, he somehow fell asleep; the road was seldom used after dark and the ground held much of the warmth of the indifferent sun of that day. When he awoke, he saw that it was dawn. A tall woman with red hair stood over him, nudging him with her foot. She seemed relieved to see that he was alive. In German, she asked him if he was a prisoner.

'*Häftling*?'

He nodded. 'I speak the English a little.'

'Come with me,' she said. 'The jerries will be here soon.'

She extended a hand and helped him to his feet. He wrapped the canvas around him like a shawl, but she took it from him.

'It will draw too much attention.'

She took him by the hand like a child, walked him up towards the crossroads, turned left, then left again into a street of cottages, and hustled him into a small one. He sat down on a chair, uncomprehending, as his hands were washed with a wet rag and a mug of parsnip coffee and a piece of real bread were placed before him. He looked at them.

'Eat,' said the woman. 'It's all right.'

He ate and drank in a trance, then started to cry. She patted him gently on the shoulder. 'It was lucky I was up early and saw you. I know what's been happening at the building site,' she said. 'You can stay here with us.'

Her name was Pauline. She was in her mid-twenties. She walked with a slight limp (my vacation in the French prison, she would joke, but sometimes she appeared to be in pain). She shared the house with Dieter, a German deserter who was her lover, and Jenny Viner, an older Jewish lady in hiding. Pauline and Dieter seemed to be active in the Resistance. Peter did not ask questions. He just accepted their food and shelter, sleeping in the cellar at night, sitting in the kitchen with Miss Viner during the day. Miss Viner had registered, but had quickly gone into hiding when she heard some terrifying early rumours. She knew her nerves would not allow her the frequent trips to the Aliens Office and God knew where else to comply with the regulations. She was terrified of being found and exiled, or worse. She had been a teacher in one of the local schools; when Peter was able to speak without crying, and she was not needed by Dieter and Pauline to help draft circulars, she helped him with his English. She would incessantly peek through the blackout curtains and then return to see if anyone had seen her peeking; the lessons suffered as a result. Except for Pauline, they all had hiding places in the house, which had a small garden but was otherwise in plain view of the neighbouring homes. In times of danger Dieter hid under the floorboards in the bedroom he shared with Pauline, Miss Viner lay under burlap sacks in the garden shed and Peter hid in the cellar. Whoever had a wireless wasn't telling, in case one of them was arrested. Pauline worked in a hotel in St Helier as a maid; she could bicycle without discomfort and set off early most mornings. It had been fortunate that she had found Peter on one of her days off. She was able to pilfer small amounts of food from time to time; many Nazi officers used this hotel, so it was well-stocked from the black market.

Eventually Peter was able to get through an entire day without crying. The terror of what he had witnessed was replaced by the lower-key, constant fear of being found out. This was the usual state of the people in hiding on the Islands; he had rejoined the ranks of the normal.

CHAPTER 38

La Rocquaise, St Brelade

April 1943

Marlene lay on her camp bed. She was listening to the BBC on the crystal set, keeping her head motionless so as not to disturb the tiny cat's whisker wire pulling in the signal. The Germans were losing in North Africa, and the RAF was bombing Berlin. More than eighty people, some of them Jews, had been sent to internment camps in February. The diphtheria outbreak was almost over. Where were the Americans? Why was she still hungry? Suzanne and Lucille had located a source of rabbit meat at a nearby farm. It was very expensive, and they didn't have much to barter for it. A small rabbit meat sandwich twice weekly was the three women's only treat. The rest of the week it was swedes, occasionally beetroot and potatoes, and potato 'bread'. For months after Marlene's mother had died, Marlene had felt a large carved-out wound in her heart, an emptiness that was the main component of her body, the rest of her curled protectively around it. Now the emptiness was a little lower, in her stomach. All her activities were devoted to meeting its needs. What activities could she perform? She was a non-person, a cipher on a camp bed in the cellar, a mouse scratching and squeaking.

She shifted in the bed and a different station came in; the faint accent told her it was a German station. They played good music; you just had to ignore the heavy-handed propaganda. She found herself listening to a broadcast for Allied soldiers in Italy, a show called *Gerry's Front*, which she had never heard before. She was astonished to hear Bruno and his Swinging Tigers play a Benny Goodman tune, 'And the Angels Sing'. It had been her mother's favourite song! It was a Jewish song! Her mother would always stop whatever she was doing and dance around the kitchen, or sitting room, or wherever she happened to be, when that song came on the wireless; she had loved swing. Marlene continued listening, horrified. Once in a while, when her mother was alive, something surprising would happen (an increase in the price of potatoes), or young Marlene would do something naughty, and her mother would say, 'Your father is spinning in his grave!' Her mother was, no doubt, spinning in Almorah right now, aghast that filthy Jew-hating pigs were playing her favourite song while her daughter was a mouse in a cellar! What about her father, with his four Jewish grandparents? Marlene couldn't remember if the song had been around when her father was alive. Was he spinning in his grave in the Jewish section, or was he happy he was dead? Bruno and the Tigers played on; Marlene thought about the lead musician, a trumpeter, who was playing his heart out. It couldn't possibly be a Nazi; she had heard enough swing, including Jewish-influenced swing, to know a Nazi couldn't possibly play it that well. Where had that trumpeter come from? One of the camps? She wanted to send something out to him, to say I know you, I know how sick this makes you, at least I'm hearing you too, and I'm Jewish enough to be hiding in a cellar, please, please be all right. She curled herself around her gnawing stomach, her aching heart, and sobbed.

CHAPTER 39

Ritz Hotel, St Helier

10th May, 1943

Tunis was lost. The officers were failing to keep up an optimistic façade; the men noted this as validation of their own fears, their growing disgust. The shining Aryan knights of the Third *Reich* were so much cannon fodder.

They sat in the mess hall/dining room of this, their billet, finishing a meal of chicken, swedes and cabbage. Their rifles rested against the chair rail.

He looked around the table at his sullen fellow guardians of *Festung Europa* – prison wardens, really. An army of prison wardens, a world of prisoners and slaves and the dead. He had had a letter from his mother; his sister had been questioned by the *Gestapo* back in Hamburg for making 'remarks'; she could be put in prison at any time.

The silence sharpened his anxiety.

'Let's have a drink, shall we?' he said.

They nodded, and he and several of his comrades rushed to bring whisky bottles out of their various hiding places.

They poured, stood, and turned to face the *Führer*'s portrait. Nobody moved, no arms raised in salute. Silence thickened in the room. They looked at one another and remained still. From now on they would always refer to events as 'before the toast' and 'after the toast'. Nobody said anything. A full minute passed; they began to chuckle nervously, make as to sit down. Still chuckling darkly over their audacity, they began to drink in silence.

Franzi started to cry.

'*Franzi, was ist loß*?' they asked. '*Franzi, wer ist die Fräulein*?'

But he knew Franzi wasn't crying over a romance.

'It's not a *Fräulein*. No *Fräulein* would want me if she knew what I had done in this war. I don't want to go back to Germany. I couldn't face my grandma after this.'

He drained his glass.

'I don't want to go back, either. I want to live in a decent country, not a place that tells us to hate everybody.'

'They sent my brother to the Eastern Front. I know he is going to die. I hate them.' More tears.

He spoke up. 'Do you remember last year, on the *Führer*'s birthday, that soldier who shot his sergeant-major while he was lecturing on the *Führer* this and the *Führer* that?'

'Yes. Then he shot himself in the lecture hall.'

'I don't want to shoot myself. I don't want to shoot anyone.'

'Sometimes I want to shoot myself, especially when I see people afraid of me.'

'What are we doing to these people? They're just town and country folk like our people in Germany. They're not monsters. They hate us. The whole world hates us.'

He nodded, picked up his glass, drained it, and hurled it at the portrait, shattering the glass in the frame. Wild with hatred and whisky, he picked up his rifle with fixed bayonet and charged the portrait, aiming for the stupid little moustache. Cheering, others followed suit; they threw the shredded picture out of the window.

They had already started setting fire to the furniture when he slipped out through a back entrance.

They found him a couple of weeks later, getting a little sun on the edge of a field. He offered no resistance. They beat him, as he knew they would. Someone smuggled a bottle of water into his cell. Before sunrise the next morning he was taken outside to the back of the prison and a shovel was placed in his hands. He knew what was coming.

He began to dig, slowly and neatly. They let him set the pace. Some tears for his sister, his mother, mixed with the soil, but his hands did not shake. He worked steadily despite the pain in his shoulder. Oddly, he found himself thinking of something he had seen on one of his infrequent visits to church. A woman, her face suffused with devotion, had sung something by Bach, 'Ich habe genug' – 'I have enough' – the words of the Virgin Mary after her purification following Jesus's birth. I have enough, he thought; I know that hate-filled monster is not my True Leader, I got a few days of freedom and sun, which is all anyone could ask for. He continued his methodical digging for a couple of hours as gulls soared in the brightening sky. Finished, he straightened up. He smiled at the guard, unnerving him. 'Ich habe genug,' he said. The shots rang out. The body, a severed marionette, tumbled into the pit.

CHAPTER 40

St Helier

June 1943

Clifford Orange and his underlings were in constant communication with the Attorney General, the Bailiff, and the *Feldkommandantur*'s office. Orange kept updating lists of people who had yet to be photographed; he communicated to Aubin about 'refractory persons', urging him to get the police involved.

Late in June, word came to him that someone had evaded his search: a Mary Erica Richardson. He vaguely remembered her name, and then, looking up his office diary from the year before, remembered that he had gone to Mrs Richardson's home in St Saviour to show her the Ninth Order; she had rebuffed him, saying that she was not Jewish, but he had thought that she was, and evidently the Germans thought so, too. He picked up the phone.

On 25 June, Mrs Richardson was helping her husband wash up after lunch. He was now mostly bedridden due to heart disease and arthritis. He was quite alert, though. Edmund knew of her predicament vis-à-vis the Jewish-registration issue. He wasn't full of advice, but he was ready to help his 'little Dutch girl', as he still called her. He thought Albert Bedane's offer of assistance was very kind, and told her to consider it.

There was a knock on the door and two men burst in. They did not identify themselves; they could have been constables or plainclothes German police, many of whom were fluent in English.

'Mrs Mary Erica Richardson?' they shouted. They did not look in the mood to take anything but a 'yes'.

'Yes?' said Mrs Richardson, gripping Edmund's hands tightly. He said nothing.

'We are ordered to take you to be photographed.'

They walked over to her and each took one of her arms, not looking at Edmund, who sat, stunned, in bed. She was hustled into the back seat of a car parked outside. The car headed west into St Helier, over to Scott's on Broad Street, the official Occupation photography studio. Passers-by tried not to look at her directly as she was pulled out of the car, in shock. She stared blankly into the camera as the flash went off. Her two escorts then took her by the arms again.

'We will take you to the *Feldkommandantur* at College House.'

She was bundled back into the rear seat and the car roared off with her sandwiched between the two men, going the several blocks east to Bagatelle Road. All this petrol for one person! At College House, she was ushered into a room; a balding man in a well-pressed uniform sat behind a desk.

'Mrs Richardson,' he said. He seemed to have a permanent sneer. 'You had not gone for your photograph. Why is that?'

'I, uh, I didn't want to.'

What was she supposed to say? Look at what they were doing to people with just one Jewish relative! She had wanted to stay out of it.

'You were ORDERED to, Mrs Richardson!' he brought his fist down on the desk, making her jump. 'Where were you born?'

This question put her at ease; she was ready for it. I must think of this as a game, she thought.

'In New Amsterdam, in British Guiana.'

He sat back and looked at her with narrowed eyes. She looked at his hands. He was wearing a wedding ring. I feel sorry for his wife, she thought. He must have a bad temper at home. He stood, went over to the corner, and picked up a globe from its stand.

'Show me!'

Fortunately Edmund, who had decided on this fictional birthplace, had shown it to her many times on the map. She pointed it out as the officer looked at her coldly.

'What were your parents' names, Mrs Richardson?' he spat.

'Mary and Howard.'

'Mary and Howard WHAT?'

'Mary and Howard Algernon.'

'We have no record that we can find of a Mary and Howard Algernon in Guiana or in Jersey.'

'Well, that is what their names were, and they did not live in Jersey. They left Guiana for Holland.'

To keep from peeing in her chair from fright, she tried to imagine him in his pyjamas. They were baggy.

'Are you a Jewess?'

'No, I am not a Jewess.'

He seemed to smirk. 'We have reason to believe you are. Because you did not register as a Jewess, and because you never had your photograph taken, you give us no choice but to deport you.'

Oh, God. Don't panic.

'But, my husband is ill … ' Albert. I have to see Albert. He can help me; he said he would.

'That does not matter. You refused to follow the orders of the *Feldkommandantur*; now you must accept your punishment.'

'Can I go home and say goodbye to my husband?'

'Go home and get enough food for forty-eight hours. You will be going on a trip.'

Two different men, clearly Germans, appeared and bundled her into the back seat of a different car.

Back in St Saviour, they escorted her through the front door. She looked at Edmund, sitting up in bed.

'Edmund, dear, they are taking me away.' Her lips contorted and let out a sob. She choked, then continued. 'I am going to get a few things. Maybe you should make some tea for our guests?'

He looked her straight in the eyes, telling her to be strong. 'Yes, dear, I'll do that.'

One of the men went to the rear of the flat with her. She took a blanket off the bed, grabbed two frocks and a jumper out of the closet, surreptitiously picked up her dark glasses and her favourite earrings.

'Tea's ready!' Edmund called.

'I'll be there soon!' she called, as if it were an ordinary day. Then she turned to her guard. 'Would you mind getting the tea and bringing it here? I still have a few things to do.'

He nodded and headed to the front of the flat. As soon as he had left the room, she was at the window. She opened the screen, threw her handbag out of the window and then stepped out herself. She started down the street as if going shopping, but then turned down an alleyway and quickly, using alleys and side streets, made her way to Albert Bedane's clinic.

It did not take long for the Germans to notice her absence. Furious, they turned to Edmund.

'Are you *Herr* Richardson?' asked one as the other began tearing around the flat, looking in clothes closets.

'What's that, boy?' The captain affected a blank look, allowed a little saliva to run out of the corner of his mouth.

'I said, are you *Herr*, or, uh, Captain Richardson?'

'No, not today, son. Today I am Captain Bligh. What do you want?'

'Where is your wife?'

'My what? My wife? What do you mean, where is my wife?'

'*Karl, er ist wahnsinnig!*' – 'He is demented!' – shouted the other man, '*Komm!*'

Karl left the captain's side and proceeded to go on a fruitless search. Edmund regarded them with contempt as they crashed around the rooms and prayed that they would leave. Finally, they did.

She tried to slow her steps and put on the dark glasses. No one seemed to be following her. When she got to the clinic she went to the back door and knocked hard; thankfully he, and not a nurse, opened it.

'Mrs Richardson! What happened?'

'Please let me in, Albert, the Germans are after me!'

'Come with me,' he said and grabbed her hand, pulling her down the hall to the basement stairs before anyone else saw them. He opened the door and revealed three rooms with low ceilings that allowed her to stand erect but made him stoop. He showed her a bed, blankets, water, a slop bucket, and brought down some bread. 'Stay here for now, dear,' he said. 'After a while perhaps you can stay in our house next door.'

Mrs Richardson burst into tears, taking his hands and holding them to her lips.

'Thank you, thank you so much!'

He looked embarrassed.

'It's all right, dear. I enjoy having a little company. My wife and daughter are back in Devon, with my wife's family.'

'But this could get you shot!'

'Well, better be shot for a sheep than a lamb, I always say.

I'll try to get you more food. My clients often pay me in food, you know, so I don't think you have to worry. My wife's clothes won't fit you, but if you know how to sew, I think you might be able to use some of them. I had better get back now, before I'm missed.'

'Thank you, Albert.'

She sat on the bed and removed her shoes. She missed Edmund already, but at least he knew where she was. Albert could probably get word to him once in a while, and see how he was doing. How long would she be here? She was so overwrought that all she could do now was sit and stare out into space. Eventually she fell asleep.

```
Attorney General's Chambers.
Jersey

26th June 1943.

[To:] The Constable of St. Peter

Dear Constable,

I understand that you were recently informed by
the Constable of St. Helier, in compliance with
an Order of the Occupying Authority, that a Mrs
Mary Erica Richardson (née Algernon) was missing
from her last registered address, 8, Overseas
Flats, Dicq Road, St. Saviour.
  I have now been requested to forward to you for
your information, and to assist you for the
purposes of identification, two copies of the
photograph of Mrs Richardson which is attached to
her registration papers.

Yours faithfully,

Charles Duret Aubin
Attorney General
```

[To:] The Constable of St. Peter.

Addendum: 2 July

Town Hall state that maiden name should read
'OLJENICH'.

CHAPTER 41

St Brelade, Jersey

8 September 1943

At seven p.m., the BBC reported that Italy had surrendered unconditionally. At the cinema later that night, everybody knew about it by intermission. As Lucille and Suzanne worked feverishly on letters, Marlene lay on her camp bed, surveying her dark world. She thought about her trumpeter. There was no need for the soft woman's voice intoning the names of American and British POWs on *Gerry's Front*; Bruno and His Swinging Tigers had nothing more to do. She felt happy for the Italians, but knew that the little wires and crystal that had connected her to the trumpeter now connected her to a prisoner, or a dead man. How had music become so dangerous? Everything was dangerous to the Nazis; she remembered them burning books from the public library shortly after the Occupation had begun. Why were Jewish people dangerous? She, for one, was harmless enough. Well, at least until she had seen Pauline in St Helier. Where was Pauline now? She had probably not spent too much time in prison; the prisons were so overcrowded with people caught hiding food, listening to the wireless, throwing manure at soldiers, that nobody stayed for long, even in France. Unless they considered your crime so grave you went to Germany; that was bad.

She imagined a prisoner exchange, Pauline for the trumpeter. Though they were both being held by the same side, weren't they? The Germans hadn't been sending out their military marching band of late; did they need a trumpeter? It was so important to be needed by them. That was how you survived. A group of anonymous prisoners became a labour pool if their work was suddenly needed. A man whose soul burned with music considered worthless pollution suddenly became bait for the hook.

Where was he now? If he was lucky, lying on a bed in a cellar like her. Probably trumpetless, practising his key fingering on air, humming when it was safe to do so. Eating rotten vegetables. If he wasn't lucky ... well, she was afraid to think about it. She wrote scenarios in her head about a trumpeter so essential to the ongoing war effort that the Nazis kept him and his family safe in a secret apartment, brought them food, brought him oil for his valves, or whatever trumpeters used. His playing was the only thing that relieved Hitler's headaches, or they thought it interfered with Allied radio transmissions (though he also played secret code that helped the RAF, and sometimes he, at great risk to his life, made the headaches worse).

She put her hands up in the darkness and fluttered her fingers as if pressing keys, playing a song to him. Then she smoothed her little pigskin blanket over her feet and tried to sleep.

CHAPTER 42

States of Jersey
Department of Public Health
Public Health Office
Royal Square
Jersey

A.M. Coutanche, Esq.
Bailiff
Bailiff's Chambers
Royal Square

Dear Sir,

I have been receiving from various sources
complaints about the feeding of political
prisoners in the gaol when under the care of our
prison staff.
  These complaints have become very insistent
since the stopping of food from outside, or
rather the reduction of this to a few kilos a
month.
  Two prisoners were on T.B. Rations before
admission, S. Coombs and J. Mackay-Tipping. I
spoke to Dr. Bentlif about these patients and I
believe he spoke to Mr Briard. Since then medical
certificates have been given to the Governor
referring to the necessity of both these men
receiving T.B. Rations. Up to the time of
writing, I am not aware that they are having
these extra rations. It would appear that much
unnecessary difficulty has been placed in the way
of these men getting the extras they require.
Both men were X-rayed and examined before
admission so that there exist a good record of
their condition then.

I have reason to believe that the following
constitutes a typical day's menu:

  Breakfast. Coffee, dry bread and swedes.
  Dinner. Soup and a small portion of potatoes.
  Tea. Coffee, dry bread, and porridge.

These men have committed no offence against our
laws, yet it would seem that they are forced to
subsist on a diet which greatly adds to the
severity of their punishment and this whilst in
charge of their fellow citizens.

   It also involves serious dangers should any of
them have latent lesions of Tuberculosis.

   There are also complaints about the amount of
fuel supplied as the political prisoners are in
that part of the gaol which has no central
heating.

Since writing the above, as a result of pressure
from Doctors Blampied and Hanna, the Governor of
the prison has asked the German Authorities for
permission to put these men on T.B. Rations. The
German Authorities have communicated with the
Attorney General who in turn has written to me
asking for my opinion. I consider all this delay
unnecessary and even the permission of the German
Authorities need not have been sought. Action
could have been taken until such time as the
German Authorities saw fit to interfere.

Yours faithfully,

R. N. McKinstry
Medical Officer of Health.

CHAPTER 43

St Helier, Jersey

October 1943

Erica Richardson had assumed a routine. She would awake early; this allowed her to use the bathroom upstairs, before the other employees had arrived. She would take her breakfast back in the cellar, allowing a block of light to come in through the little window by opening the blackout curtain but of course not sitting in direct view. She would walk a few laps around her bed after making it up to stretch her legs. Then she would light a candle to supplement the window and sew. She was getting the hang of it: her first efforts on Mrs Bedane's clothes were laughable, but she quickly realized that one sewed things inside out. Soon she was able to alter a few skirts and blouses so that she could deal with the long drying time required for doing secret indoor laundry. She would take lunch in the cellar as well, always brought down by Albert. After the employees had all left and the blackout curtains were closed, she would sometimes have dinner with him upstairs.

As they gnawed on dry, pan-scorched swedes (no butter was at hand at the moment for frying) and potato bread, he spoke up.

'Erica,' he said (she had insisted he call her that), 'I think it has been long enough now that nobody would recognise you if they saw you for a moment.'

'You think so?'

'Yes. I think you may be able to move into the house. We have an upstairs bedroom with heavy curtains that I think

147

would be all right. After another few months, maybe you could sit in the garden if you wore your dark glasses and maybe dyed your hair.'

She laughed. 'That sounds funny. I would have to be more glamorous in order to not be recognised!'

'I didn't mean that you weren't … '

'Oh, Albert, I know! It's just funny. What did Edmund say to you the other day?'

'That if I touched his little Dutch girl, he would keelhaul me!'

'We've all grown so emaciated, never mind our ages, you couldn't do the former and he couldn't do the latter!'

'I'm afraid you're right. Listen, another reason I need to move you is that I may be taking in a Frenchman or a Russian worker.'

'Really?'

'My little circle of friends tells me that there are several people in need of a hiding place. The Germans torture those Russians terribly, you know. They beat them and starve them to death.'

'I've heard that. It's terrible.'

'Well, I just wanted to let you know so you wouldn't be surprised.'

'Thank you, Albert. I'll try to tidy up the cellar for the next guest.'

Another thing to occupy her time. Hoping against hope, she wondered if Albert would get two people at the same time so they could play cards.

His name was Oleg. He was smuggled in at night. She met him the next day, after he had had a bath and a little food. He looked terrible! His scalp was half-bald and scabby, his frame devoid of flesh, his teeth rotten. He had already been at another hiding place, where he had been de-loused and given some ill-fitting clothes; God knew what he had looked like when he escaped. He did not talk much and knew just a little English.

She sat up in her new room, a slightly stuffy bedroom with all-over heavy curtains lined with net. She had the use of a bathroom now. She asked Albert for some of his own clothes to alter for the Russian. This sewing was becoming agreeable to her. She sat on her bed during the shortening days and sewed. She embroidered her pillowcases with thread unravelled from too-long trousers. At night she listened to a forbidden wireless hidden under a wastebasket; it certainly sounded as though the Allies were getting things done in Italy. Albert was able to bring her word and the occasional note from her husband, who was getting a bit weaker but still able to care for himself with a little help from the neighbours. She did not think about the obvious: if we are ever found out, we will all be shot, or sent to a camp where even worse things are done to you. The thought could make her crazy; she became adept at not thinking it and just looking ahead to her next frugal meal.

CHAPTER 44

St Brelade, Jersey

1 June 1944

Fitful weather all spring, planes roaring overhead, soldiers mutinying, nightly German target practice. In May, several airdrops of radio-scrambling foil-backed paper occurred, courtesy of the RAF. On one was scrawled 'Don't worry, Jersey, won't be for long.' Later that month, attacks on St Aubin's Bay. People were nervous, shyly optimistic, searching one another's emaciated faces for information.

That evening Lucille and Suzanne were listening to the wireless set hidden in Lucille's ottoman, one to an earphone; Marlene was listening to her crystal set in the cellar. After the opening notes of Beethoven's Fifth Symphony, the European News Service announcer began the news by saying, 'Here is the news, but first here are some messages for our friends in occupied countries:

The long sobbing of the violins of Autumn,
Molasses tomorrow will spurt forth cognac,
Sabine ...'

The sisters looked at each other, then hugged, crying, 'The Verlaine! The Verlaine!' The line about violins, the first line of Paul Verlaine's *Chanson d'Automne*, was the signal to the Resistance to make ready for the Allied invasion of France.

Marlene in her cellar heard the nonsense sentences, but did

not understand what they meant. She sat up when Lucille came down.

'Marlene, things will happen now. We are very excited.'

'What things?'

'We cannot tell you everything, but good things will happen, dear. Do not worry.'

The next day was filled with the clacking of the typewriter.

CHAPTER 45

La Rocquaise, St Brelade, Jersey

5 June 1944

The Trojan War will not be held.
John is growing a very long beard this week.
The long sobbing of the violins of Autumn
Les sanglots longs des violins de l'automne
Wound my heart with a monotonous languor …

'From the Italian front, a late bulletin reports … '

Before the announcer had finished reading the second line of the Verlaine, the line they had been waiting for, Lucille wriggled out of her half of the headphones. She threw on a wig and a coat, kissed Suzanne, and slipped out through the back door. Suzanne sat at the table in the dark, smoking, listening to the little wireless. Planes were taking off from England, laden with paratroopers. Rome had been liberated. She put the set away carefully after the broadcast, returned to her place at the table, waiting for Lucille, allowing herself another precious cigarette. Lucille returned as night was turning to day, and sat again at the table. In the old days Lucy would have been giddy with excitement, but now she wearily reported on tyre slashings, artillery sabotage and dynamite theft.

'They have shut down the telephone lines,' she said, unsure if this was good or bad, 'I think the *Kommandant* will be making a proclamation. A lot of the Germans seem pretty happy, though. They are sick of this.'

The thundering drone of planes overhead began, and

continued all day, louder and louder, punctuated by antiaircraft fire from the nearby emplacements. When the windows began to vibrate with the growing percussive roar, they went downstairs to where Marlene was somehow sleeping through the noise.

'Marlene,' said Suzanne, shaking her awake, 'the invasion has begun.'

They brought the second crystal wireless down to the cellar and heard General Eisenhower announce the beginning of their liberation. That evening they heard the King address the Empire and most of the rest of the world. Obviously reading, and haltingly, from a text, he made the expected call for prayer and fortitude. Marlene had never heard him before. They tried to make a little party in the cellar, eating swedes and drinking wine and parsnip coffee as young men flew their large aeroplanes towards Normandy.

CHAPTER 46

St Helier, Jersey

5 June 1944

Erica lay awake in the upstairs bedroom, listening to the drone of planes between broadcasts on the wireless. This was an exciting moment; the Allies were invading from France. Perhaps the war would end soon; a thought that was probably in everyone's mind. She missed her husband terribly; she knew he was all right, but she longed to see him. Oleg was looking much better; he was almost dapper in the clothes she had altered for him. They would all eat dinner together on Sunday evenings, when there was no risk of being seen by employees, and Albert would bring out the best food given to him by his patients. Afterwards they would sometimes play cards; she looked forward to this the most. The little risks and losses of the games took her mind off the risks of impending capture and execution. All this because of her little Jewish grandfather! He asked her to call him *'zayde'*, taught her bits of Yiddish (her mother was horrified that he taught her some words that were not very nice), gave her rides on his back. That was what she remembered of him; he died when she was ten. Now she was fifty-five, grey-haired, a little arthritic, and a fugitive from the Nazis. The world was so crazy!

CHAPTER 47

La Rocquaise, St Brelade, Jersey

June 1944

Armed soldiers were deployed everywhere; the ugly wounds of trenches filled the parks and fields. Planes roared overhead, sometimes all night as well as all day. The Germans grew increasingly tense, the citizens increasingly hopeful. Lucille and Suzanne took stock of their food supplies; the sources from France were now cut off, and Germans and citizens would be scrounging for the same potatoes and bread. Rations were cut down three weeks after the invasion. People were arrested, fined, and jailed for minor infractions. Ships left St Helier with German evacuees, then returned when Allied vessels were sighted. Some ships limped in after being damaged by bombs and torpedoes. The phone was still forbidden, the beaches off limits. Lucille and Suzanne listened to the wireless, scribbled excitedly on their tissue paper, dropped their missives, waited. Marlene lay sleepless in her cellar. She was waiting for a soldier to come running down the stairs, a British soldier, holding chocolate bars and fruit, pulling her off the camp bed and dancing with her, telling her it was all over, she could come out now, she could find a job and a new flat and be a human being again. But every time someone came down, it was Lucille or Suzanne with swedes and parsnip coffee and words of encouragement that, like the meal itself, never cheered her more than momentarily. The aeroplanes were real, the news on the BBC was real, but so were the visits to Suzanne and then to Lucille by the *Geheime Feldpolizei*, the

155

secret military police, for interrogation. They tried to laugh it off, but Marlene could see the toll it was taking on them, the exhaustion and fear in their eyes, in unguarded moments.

CHAPTER 48

La Rocquaise, St Brelade, Jersey

June 1944

The noise of a car engine was heard outside. Suzanne and Lucille sat at the table, set with silver and handmade pottery, a swede and a potato each on their plates. They dropped their forks when they saw the official car stop outside their house. Suzanne stamped on the floor to warn Marlene. Lucy was just starting to run up the stairs when, hardly taking time to knock, two officers rushed in. They recognised *Oberleutnant* Lung, who pulled Lucy back down the stairs and pushed her into a chair. The other officer went upstairs and Lung stayed with them on the first floor. Soon, the officer came down with the typewriter and wireless from Lucy's ottoman. Suzanne berated herself. We must have left the earphone out. Well, the typewriter is bad enough.

'You are now under arrest, and must come to headquarters.'

Lucy fainted and slid to the floor. Suzanne stood up.

'I'll get her some water.'

Lung nodded. Suzanne got a glass of water and slowly introduced it to Lucy's lips as she woke up. Lucy looked around, and then shot a look of pure and fiery love to Suzanne, who squeezed her hand and fought back tears. Then she stood up.

'My sister has a bad heart. She needs her tablets.'

'Very well, get them,' was Lung's reply.

Suzanne ran upstairs and grabbed two bottles of sleeping pills, hiding one in her trouser pocket. She showed the other to Lung.

'She needs two of these every night.'

'We will see to it,' he said, taking the bottle.

Lucille and Suzanne sat, holding hands tightly, in the back of the big car, which smelled of cigarette smoke. Lung sat next to them. The unfamiliar officer drove. The car, doubtless requisitioned from one of Jersey's wealthier citizens, purred down the road but still bounced them up and down over the yawning potholes that nobody troubled to fill in. On a particularly rough stretch, Suzanne pulled the top off the bottle in her pocket and emptied the pills into her hand. Feigning a cough, she pushed half the amount into her mouth and somehow managed to give Lucille the rest without Lung noticing. They sat there trying to swallow the bitter tablets with saliva without tipping-off the officers. A glance of triumph passed between them. Suzanne found herself thinking, of all things, of the Love-Death scene from *Tristan and Isolde*. She had never liked Wagner much, though Lucy did. Her body began to feel so heavy she did not know how she would get out of the car, but they both managed it when the unfamiliar officer (Lung called him 'Sarmsen') pulled into the drive of Gloucester Street Prison. Lucy exuded a calm that did not seem to have anything to do with the pills. She stood up straight, fighting the void, her blue eyes luminous.

It was very late, and after a perfunctory check-in they were ushered into a cell with a mattress, where, rapidly becoming stuporous, they sank down, hands tightly joined, and awaited deliverance. Lucy tried to tell Suzanne that she hoped Suzanne felt as good about her life's work as she, Lucille, did, but the words stuck on her thick tongue and she was content to melt into Suzanne's side, smell her smell, and rob the Nazis of their latest prize.

CHAPTER 49

St Brelade, Jersey

July 1944

The tapping on the ceiling was unmistakable; the pattern that they had agreed upon to mean 'Danger! Get out!' Marlene's blood froze. Lucille (she thought) tapped the pattern twice; then there was silence. It sounded as though they were in the front room, taking attention away from her to aid her escape. She grabbed the radio bag and tiptoed up the cellar stairs. She couldn't see them. Muttering a silent prayer, she lifted her coat off its nail and slipped out the back door. She was in luck; the *Geheime Feldpolizei* had not surrounded the house but were simply entering by the front door. All the same, their arrest was likely.

Head down, hands in her pockets, she walked slowly and in a roundabout way to the coastal road. Lucille and Suzanne, leaving nothing to chance, had drilled this procedure into her. It was so automatic that she could do it while at first numb, and then choked with grief and fear. It was a hot evening, and it didn't look like rain. If she raised suspicion by wearing a coat, she was doomed. But these days, nobody asked too many questions or took the trouble to report anything; they were too busy trying to fill their bellies. There were plenty of people who walked around with looks of anguish; whose loved ones were in internment camps, whose children learned German on empty stomachs, who lived in fear of their own government officials, who had seen neighbours turn into thieves and traitors.

Marlene walked down the road and tried to think without

crying. She dared not go back for her bicycle. Her tea was long gone; she couldn't use it for bribes. She did have some money, handkerchiefs, underwear, the cup. She did not know how long it was till curfew. She had to get to some kind of shelter before one of the Germans stopped her and demanded her papers; if he wouldn't take a bribe, she would be arrested. Then what? She kept walking. Thin, grey, unhappy people were everywhere. Their outside source of food, France, had been cut off by the invasion of Normandy.

She turned up a side street going away from the coast; she had to hide. She needed to find an abandoned building; she didn't want to call attention to any of Lucille and Suzanne's friends by showing up on their doorstep. In the fading light, a couple of miles up the road, near the fortifications and the labour camp, she saw an obviously abandoned farmhouse. It was dangerous to squat in these houses; the neighbours might inform on you, and the Germans might inspect it.

She made her way to the back of the house, where the requisite shed stood, its door hanging crookedly from one hinge. This one was long and narrow; perhaps it had housed chickens. She stood still for a dangerously long time, looking at it. Her adult life had had two stages. The first, as a clerk in the Aliens Office, had been stable, if dull. Then had come the punctuation of an overnight stay in a chapel, then her emergence as Marlene, farmworker and Resistance member. Would this shed be another punctuation mark, or rather another incubator from which would emerge a third Marlene? She wanted to continue in the Resistance, but knew she had to lie very low now. Well, she was good at that.

She sighed and walked up to the door, which opened out at a crazy angle. She walked in and closed the door behind her. One small window at each end allowed a smeary light. A heap of straw smelling of animal dung took up the floorspace to her left; on the right, a heap of rags took up a small amount of room. She kicked the straw, trying to see where the droppings were; there didn't seem to be any, but it smelled so vile she decided to throw it out of the door. That done, she looked at the pile of rags. To her horror, it started to move. She screamed. A head popped out of the pile; it had wild hair and few teeth.

'Please! Please! Quiet! Miss, please quiet!'

It was a man with a foreign accent; it did not sound German, but she couldn't stop shaking.

'I'm sorry,' she said. 'I didn't know you were under there. I'll leave. Don't worry, I won't say anything.'

'You live here, miss?' A scrawny leg extended from the pile.

'No, I don't.'

'Why you come in here? Please, I do not hurt you.' A hand followed.

'I came in here to hide. They arrested the people I was staying with.'

'Oh, that is bad. So you are hiding, too.' Then, the formalities completed, 'Do you have any food?'

'No, uh, yes, uh, let me look.' She felt in her pockets, which she had always kept replenished. She found some dried swede slices. She handed them to the man.

'Oh, miss, thank you. I no eat for two days. You have for you, too.'

'No, it's all right. I ate today.'

'No, miss, you take one.'

'No, really. It's all right. I, I'm too upset to eat it. You have it, please.'

'Thank you again.' The bony hand crammed the slices into the partly toothless mouth.

'You're welcome.' She began to open the door. 'I'm sorry I

surprised you. I'll go somewhere else.' Where, she didn't know. Her legs were shaking so hard she couldn't walk much.

'Wait, miss.'

The man sat up; sitting, he finally looked like a human being and not like a collection of limbs and rags. He was very thin, with a complexion even more unhealthy than that of most of the half-starved Jerseymen. Marlene realised he must be an escaped prisoner from one of the notorious labour camps. She knew of the informal network of safe houses for them; lately many of them had been raided and the locals running them sent to different camps from the ones the British-born had been sent to. If they were anything like the slave labour camps on Jersey, they were nightmarish.

'Wait, miss, please,' he said again. 'It is good here, is safe. Do you want water?' He extended a stoppered bottle half-filled with water.

'Thank you.'

She drank a few swallows, took a deep breath. She was still shaking. He took the bottle back and finished it.

'Are you from the prison camp?' she asked.

'Yes, miss. I escape from *Lager* Himmelman. It was very bad.'

She knew that if his English vocabulary were more extensive, he would have chosen more – and different – words.

'I stay at a lady's house for six months, then they arrest her a few months ago.'

His mouth twisted, and tears glistened in his eyes before he blinked them away.

Her tears answered his. 'I escaped from St Helier a few years ago; I stayed with two ladies for a long time. They were arrested this morning.'

'Oh, miss, they are crazy animals! What is your name, miss?'

'Marlene.' She sat down beside him, trying to stop crying.

'Marlene,' he repeated, his accent making it sound like a different name. 'I am Peter.'

'Hello, Peter.'

He began picking up stray rags.

'Please, Marlene, take some for you.'

She did not expect this. She did not know if she should be sharing a filthy shed with this scarecrow man. What should she be doing? If she declined his offer, and set out in search of another shed, she could be picked up. Without papers, with a radio (she couldn't bear to part with it), she could wind up in a camp.

She accepted the rags from him, flattened them on the floor, and sat down. They began to talk about food. Peter had been slipping out at night to steal or forage from farms. He had not been able to go out for the past two nights because, as far as she could understand his broken English, the Nazis had sent out extra patrols.

'We can go to the farm I was staying at,' she said, 'but not yet. I'm worried they are watching it. I know some other farms where they leave food for prisoners.'

'Oh, that is good. We can go there after dark. Thank you, Marlene. I am very happy you came in here.'

She managed a smile.

'Excuse me, Marlene. I am going to sleep again. It is good to sleep in day, and wake in night.'

'Yes, you're right.'

She made herself as comfortable as possible on the rags as the sun climbed higher, heating the shed. She was probably going to catch lice from his rags. She would just have to get used to it.

CHAPTER 50

Jersey Hospital, St Helier

July 1944

She tried to move her feet, but the armour was confining, and the ankle-deep water in the well numbed her up to her knees. Although at the bottom of the well, she was able to see, and had removed the gauntlet and chainmail glove from her right hand so as to hold the pistol. If she shot straight up, after an eternity, as she squeezed her eyes closed and gritted her teeth in anticipation, the bullet came singing back down the well-shaft and bounced painfully off her helmet or the armour on her shoulder. If she shot at an angle, however, the ricochet, although deafening, would send the bullet out at an angle, and sometimes she heard someone scream and blood ran down the walls of the well. She stood in the cold soup of blood and spent bullets for hours, shivering, figuring trajectories and firing up at various angles, listening for screams, other shots, catching the occasional soaring of violins. Birds in flight over the well gave her a momentary glimpse of the motion she craved, creatures going from one place to another, sure of the sustenance that awaited them, unaware of human blood. Her supply of bullets, at first coming out of nowhere, began to dwindle. She reached down and began to fish spent bullets out of the red water, feeding them back into the hungry maw of the pistol, wiping the salt and dried blood from the chamber. Eventually she used up all the bullets she could find; she felt around in the water and came up with a small fish that looked at her brightly, then cast its eyes upwards. Something was being lowered into the well; it was Lucy! She was dressed in her coquettish 'Bluebeard's Wife' costume from the Birot play she had acted in, her hair unwigged and newly golden, sitting on a platform like a child's swing, leaning on one of the ropes and touching the walls with a curious hand as she slowly descended. Finally, she slid off her swing and stood in the cold water, oblivious to the red staining her gown, and looked at Suzanne with adoring eyes. 'My Tristan, you breathe! You are slowly coming alive to me, beloved!' Only Suzanne's right hand and face were uncovered by armour. Lucy grasped her hand, kissed it, and then leaned up to kiss her lips. As she kissed her, she quickly inserted a finger into Suzanne's nostril, causing her to flinch.

Suzanne reached up to her nose and found her hand restrained. Someone had put lead weights on her eyelids. She concentrated on lifting them for several minutes, letting the rest of her body go slack. Finally, the lids parted and she then concentrated on focusing. After an hour or a day, she looked around and found herself in a hospital bed. Curtains concealed the rest of the room from her; it was silent. The finger in her nose was a rubber tube; another tube dripped watery fluid from a bottle into her left arm. She drew on a tiny store of strength and managed a cough; her tongue felt like a loaf of dry bread in her mouth. After another week or minute, she managed to croak, ''ucee, 'ucee!'

Silence. That's right, she thought, we're supposed to be dead. Are we dead? Am I dead? I don't think I am dead. Where is Lucy? After a few more furlongs of time, someone entered the room; Suzanne made her croaking sound and the curtains were parted, revealing a nurse.

'Oh, you are awake. I will get you water.'

'Where i' 'ucee? 'e alive?'

165

'Miss Schwob? Yes, she is alive. She is still asleep.' The old woman put a wet cloth to Suzanne's lips; she took the moisture greedily. 'If you can stay awake, I'll ask Dr Lewis to take that tube out of your nose.'

'My nose. Yeh, 'ake it ou'.'

She struggled mightily to keep her eyes open. The nurse returned at some point, and started to feed her spoonfuls of mashed swede. You couldn't get away from them. She found she could swallow despite the tube. Some time later, after dark, a thin man in a civilian suit came in and quickly whipped the tube out of her nose, apologising afterwards.

'It hurts less if it's done fast. I'm sorry, Miss Malherbe.' Dr Lewis leaned closer and whispered, 'I think Miss Schwob will wake up tomorrow. I know what happened. I think I can keep you here several more days.'

'Then what?'

'Then they are taking you back to the jail.' Seeing Suzanne's anguished expression, he added: 'I don't think they will do anything besides question you, Miss Malherbe. They know the war is going badly, and anything they do will be held against them when it is over. Please don't try what you did again.'

'Thank you.'

Feeling more awake, she looked around through the parted curtains. She seemed to be alone in some kind of store room. It had been a small ward, the one where the diabetics had slowly died, waiting in vain for insulin. Nobody wanted to enter the room after that.

Her wrists were tied to the bed. The nurse came back with a bedpan, which she used gratefully.

'How is Lucille?'

'Still sleeping, but I think she will be all right.'

'Can I see her when she wakes up?'

'I don't know, *mademoiselle*. They are guarding you as prisoners.'

'I understand.'

She slept, and woke, and ate mashed swede with sips of milk, and used the bedpan, and slept, until one day the nurse stood over her with her clothing, such as it was. She dressed quickly, then was escorted by a soldier to a car. Lucy was in the back! Suzanne was made to sit in the front, and talking was forbidden, but the sound of each other's little coughs was the most reassuring thing in the world. Once again, they were taken to Gloucester Street Prison.

CHAPTER 51

Gloucester Street Prison, Military Wing, St Helier, Jersey

July 1944

OFFICIAL RULES

The detainee may wear the uniform, boots, and
cap, and may keep only the following in his
possession: paybook, identity papers, bandages,
decontamination tablets, handkerchief, watch, and
wedding ring.
 Strictly forbidden: entertainment, smoking,
reading, or writing/incising on the walls of the
cell.
 Detainees can officially report rank, name,
unit, sentence, and reason for their sentence.
 Boots are to be worn during the day.
Headcovering shall be worn outside the cell.
 The detainee may shave in the morning.
 The cells and the hallway shall always be kept
clean. Trash should be placed in the appropriate
receptacles in the hallway, never in the water
closets.
 Prison-issue blankets will be removed from
cells containing blankets brought by the
detainees.
 Outside exercise in the form of brisk marching
is allowed with a three-metre distance between
detainees. It is forbidden to use this time for
sitting or putting hands in pockets.
 In the event of an Island alarm, every detainee
shall proceed as quickly as possible to the unit
from which he was arrested.

===

UNOFFICIAL RULES

As in all prisons, cigarettes are legal tender, even counterfeit ones made from coltsfoot or other handy herbs.

The guards, for the most part, aren't malicious; the officers are.

The officers reserve the right to beat, rape, torture and kill military prisoners. Between sessions, the prisoners are still allowed exercise, provided they keep their hands out of their pockets.

Don't let on to the officers that Germany is losing the war; although they know this, it helps them (and you) to preserve the fiction that each setback is only temporary. This does not apply to the guards, who get all their news from the civilian prisoners with relatives on the outside; they know the *Reich* is fucked.

Share your visitors' parcels, especially with the doomed.

Even though you are filthy, hungry, and will be freezing cold in the upcoming autumn, winter and spring; even though you have fleas and maybe lice and are beginning to worry about that bit of blood you keep coughing up; even though nice young kids are being executed after being tortured for just talking about desertion, WHATEVER YOU DO, DON'T AT-TEMPT SUICIDE. Chances are, you will make it through the winter and the *Reich* won't. Plus we need our razors.

They were each put into solitary confinement and interrogated separately. The passing of notes was impossible at first, though Lucy could occasionally catch Suzanne giving a hand signal out of her second-storey cell window when the light was good (in August, a 'V' to signal the liberation of Paris).

Although they were in military prison, and were scheduled for a court martial, they were still treated with the odd deference shown Islanders even in the most degrading conditions, plus more deference because they were rather well-known as long-time Island residents. Lucille concluded that, instead of being tortured, they would be 'shot in style or deported'.

The prison warden, Otto, who looked as though he would be a beefy sort if he had an adequate diet, regarded Lucille as she examined the pewter washbasin and tin mug in her assigned cell.

'Lady Schwob,' he began.

'*Nicht korrekt, nicht gut Englisch*,' she snapped in heavily accented German. 'Say "Miss Schwob", if you will be correct.'

He managed a '*Fräulein*' or two, then just called her '*die Kleine*', which was in a way good, because she knew the taller Suzanne was '*die Große*', and the linking of their names afforded a kind of intimacy.

Prisoners would, upon awakening, be escorted to the bathroom with their basins, to fill them at the bath tap. The sink did not work. The basins were so heavy and the prisoners so weak that to fill them more than halfway was to ask for trouble. They seldom had soap. The stench of the bathroom was cut by a small opening in the wall allowing air and a view of the outside, something they could capture and hold onto for the rest of the day, to feed their dreams as their bodies wasted. A few words could also be exchanged. Three times a day they had swede soup and potato bread with *ersatz* coffee. Often gruel, some milk, and the occasional piece of tripe. They were not allowed writing instruments or paper, but most were able to improvise.

CHAPTER 52

St Brelade, Jersey

July 1944

Marlene awoke first. She stood and looked out of the grimy window; it was almost dusk. She put her shoes on and opened the door, crept around to the far side of the building, and peed. She thought back to Suzanne and Lucille's discovery of her in the cemetery chapel. How were they, she wondered. Were they being sent to Germany? She could not think about anything worse, like execution. She saw them sharing a cell, subsisting on swedes and water, drawing armadillos and saxophones on the wall of the cell with a stolen stub of pencil.

She returned to the shed and woke Peter. For the first time he stood up in front of her; his emaciation was a stab in her heart. He looked apologetic. He wore a shirt and trousers that were too big for him; the trousers were held up by a piece of rope. A rag bandaged one ankle.

'I come back soon, Marlene.'

He opened the door clumsily, carrying his water bottle. Five minutes later it was growing dark; she heard him fumbling with the door.

'Do you want some more water? I get it from stream.'

'Yes, thank you.'

'Look.' He dug into his shirt pocket and took out a thumbnail-sized piece of soap. 'Please, you take it.'

How could she refuse? She had been bathing with ashes and lard for weeks. She took the soap, splashed some water into her hands, washed her face, and gave the tiny piece back.

'Thank you. It's so refreshing.'

They set out in the moonlight, Marlene leading the way. She took him to a farm near *La Rocquaise*. He whispered, 'It is not safe to look for food they give us now. We should dig it.' They edged onto a field, their eyes scanning in the dim moonlight for the leaves of a swede or potato. Marlene found a stunted cabbage; Peter, some beetroot in the next plot. They carried these back to the shed, where the vegetables were devoured.

'If we have luck,' said Peter, 'we will find a rat.'

'You mean, to eat it?'

'Yes. The meat, it is good. I am even sometimes able to make a little fire.'

Marlene was horrified, but said nothing. She had helped slaughter a pig in the bath, but not a rat. She had never experienced hunger like that. What other horrors had he been through? She tried not to think about it. Not thinking about things had become an important survival skill.

They fell into a routine, sleeping during the day, foraging at night. To their relief, the extra patrols seemed to have ended and some brave householders again left food out for escaped prisoners, so the occasional piece of cheese or rabbit leg kept them from eating rats. They tried foraging at *La Rocquaise*, but quickly exhausted the garden.

He told her stories after they ate. She was surprised to hear of his several prison stints, usually for demonstrating against Marshal Pilsudski. He and his comrades had been fixtures on Muranowska Street and other areas of Jewish Warsaw, slipping into factories at lunchtime to agitate for the Polish Communist Party, arguing with Bundists and Zionists, gesturing over their well-thumbed copies of the *Literary Monthly*.

Marlene picked up some pieces of wire and began trying to get the crystal set to work. One night she succeeded. One of the newsreaders was talking about something happening in the Pacific. She called Peter over, took the earphone out of her ear, and pressed it into his. She could almost hear him smile.

'Oh, is good! Is BBC? Oh, they speak so fast!'

'Sometimes they play music. The German stations play a lot of music, and you don't need to understand their English. It's all rubbish.'

'Oh, I want to hear music!'

Tears filled her eyes. How long had it been since this man had heard music? She fiddled with the coil but found no music broadcast. She found she was filled with the desire to be kind to him, in a way different from her kindness to Lucille and Suzanne.

The next day, while he slept in his pile of rags, she connected several pieces of wire together into one long strand and looped it around the doorway, keeping the shorter ground piece attached to a stake in the corner. She gently ran the pin along the coil and heard several promising bursts of static. That night, after they had returned with a cabbage and a piece of cheese, she tried again and brought in German Overseas Radio with Charlie and his Orchestra. She called him over. They lay prone on the floor, taking turns listening to the catchy cabaret tunes, ignoring the hateful content. He was entranced; it was so difficult not to hum along. When their necks were both stiff from the rock-steady position demanded by the little crystal set, they retreated to their respective sides of the shed and slept. Marlene felt a secret joy that she had restored something so intensely missed by this miserable man.

CHAPTER 53

St Brelade, Jersey

July 1944

The next night there was no moon, and clouds covered the stars.

'We cannot go to the farms tonight. We will be lost,' Peter whispered.

'We don't have any food.'

'I saved beetroot. We can drink water. Also, we can go to the stream and have bath.'

'Isn't it dangerous?'

'No people will see. It is too dark.'

They certainly needed baths. They had been able to only wash their hands and faces occasionally with water and the vanishingly small piece of soap. There was nothing they could do about the lice.

Peter had washed two pieces of canvas the day before, and they hung drying in the stuffy shed. These would serve as towels. After a repast of beetroot and water, they slipped out and walked slowly and clumsily in total darkness to the stream. Marlene carried a surprise, a small tablet of soap she had found in a handkerchief deep in the lining of her coat.

They stepped into the cool water, knee-deep, standing awkwardly, several feet apart. Marlene decided to show him the soap; she did not want to risk losing it by tossing it. She assumed he was still dressed, as she was, and was startled when she touched bare skin. He gave a little jump.

'I found this,' she whispered, grasping his hand and slipping the soap into his palm.

'Oh, Marlene, thank you!'

'Here, let me wash your hair.'

She playfully splashed water on his hair and soaped it up.

'Wait.' He reached forward in the darkness, grasped her shoulders, and then began to unbutton her blouse. 'I will wash your clothes. Is all right?'

Is it all right? She found she wanted him to touch her, she suddenly wanted it very much. Especially him, this man who shared his water, his foraged vegetables, his soap with her. This man who was made so happy by music. She smiled.

'Yes, it is all right.'

He removed her blouse, then her skirt and, with her whispered consent, her underwear. He quickly soaped and rinsed them along with his own clothes, feeling for a grassy part of the stream bank to put them down. She stood shivering in the water. Then she felt him steadying her with one hand on her shoulder while the other wet and soaped her hair. He lifted her up suddenly with a strength neither imagined he had, braced her back on his knee, and rinsed her hair as she suppressed squeals at the coldness of the water. He stood her back on her feet and washed her face. He then put the bar of soap in his mouth and spat it out, rinsing his mouth. Then he kissed her, lightly on the forehead and then hungrily on the mouth. She was astonished at the heat that rose out of her, the sudden need to feel his closeness. He soaped his hands and washed her neck, her back, her breasts. He gave her the soap and she began to lather him, starting with his face. They both were aware of each other's rank odours giving way to the faint scent of the soap, of the quiet stream, of the night breeze. She caressed each bone in his poor, thin back. She lathered his chest, buried her face in the sudsy hair, drew him close. She soaped his navel, loved the thin line of hair below it. He gently guided her hand

175

down, feeling that it would be impolite to wash his own sex in front of her, though it was dark. She soaped the hard part and the soft parts, thrilled to touch them, feeling his breath on her forehead. Then he took the soap from her, again lathering her breasts with the cold-hardened nipples until she moaned and swayed on her feet, then slipped his hand down to her softness. She was already honey-drenched but he splashed cool water onto her and took up the soap, lathering as she leaned against him. When had he last felt something so soft? Abruptly he took his hand away.

'Let us wash the soap off,' he said, and, holding hands, they squatted together so the flowing water reached up almost to their necks. Water-cleansed, love-drenched, they gathered up their clean clothes and felt their way back to the shed. Peter tossed their clothes haphazardly onto the makeshift clothesline and removed the canvas, spreading it on the floor in the darkness. She found his hands, clasped and kissed them. Then they were on the canvas. She was urgently hungry for him, to join souls and bodies after so much terrible loneliness. She was unafraid; she was not, she could not, be afraid to love. He pulled her close.

'Is all right, sweet Marlene?' he whispered hoarsely.

'Oh, Peter, yes, please.'

She felt stretched, and then united with him. Everything that had been closed and separated and muffled was open and joined and glistening. They were one clean, sweet-smelling skin; then he suddenly shuddered and collapsed upon her, weeping. After a while he rolled on his side and dried her own tears with his finger, slipping it into her mouth, then drawing a line down the contour of her body, lingering in her navel, and then down into the nectary velvet. She nuzzled into his chest as he caressed her until she found herself lifted, as if in a tiny boat on a great heartstopping swell; then she was thrown from the boat and showered with dazzling diamonds and enveloped by the softest down, somehow all at the same time. She sank back, exhausted.

CHAPTER 54

Gloucester Street Prison

July 1944

First Interrogation

Major Lohse was the officer in charge of their upcoming court martial. Tall, with greasy, colourless hair and tiny blue eyes behind round glasses, he had a detached air. He seemed pre-occupied by other matters. Well, it's better than zeal, Lucy thought as she sat in the chair, waiting for the session to begin. Lohse sat with another soldier whose name was never revealed; she thought of him as the Unknown Soldier. A nurse sat behind her. They were waiting for the interpreter, a short, ragged officer, who rushed in, saluted, and sat in front of her.

The *Major* removed his glasses and looked at Lucy. He said something softly in German and glanced at the interpreter. 'Please state your full name.'

'Lucy Renée Mathilde Schwob.'

'Where were you born?'

'In Nantes.'

'Where is that?'

'In France.'

'Where do you live now, Miss Schwob?'

'Right here, in Gloucester Street Prison.'

He seemed unfazed by this little impertinence.

'No, I mean prior to your arrest.'

'*La Rocquaise* in St Brelade.'

'Did you have a printing press in *La Rocquaise*?'

'No.'

'Did you have a typewriter?'

'Yes.'

'Did you have occasion to buy large amounts of coloured tissue paper?'

Oh, I know the bitch who ratted on us, she thought. The one we bought the paper from.

'Yes, occasionally.'

'For what purpose?'

'To write letters.'

'Letters to whom?'

'To various people.'

'Did you write to soldiers?'

'Yes.'

'Did you write letters as "*Der Soldat Ohne Namen*?"'

'Yes.'

'Did you write a poem as "Colonel Heine"?'

'Well, I *adapted* a poem by Heinrich Heine called "The Lorelei".'

The interpreter frowned. Many Germans knew the poem, but not its author, who was Jewish. The *Major* recited the last stanza of the poem, about a beautiful siren who lures sailors to their death with song, in English himself, without the interpreter. It was useful to know that he had a good facility with English.

'"I think that the waves finally swallowed up the boatman and his boat / That is what the Lorelei did with her singing."'

'That's a very good translation. Of the original, that is.'

The *Major*, finding himself flattered by a Jew on his translation of German poetry by a Jew, coloured slightly. Nobody else said anything.

'But you wrote in German, and I translate: "I think that the waves finally swallowed up the boatman and his boat / That is what Adolf Hitler did with his bellowing."'

She observed the facial expressions of the Unknown Soldier and the interpreter. The interpreter was exerting a mighty effort to keep a poker face; to chuckle right now could be fatal. The stonefaced Unknown Soldier was probably an informant for the secret police.

'I'm sorry, it rhymes better in German.'

'Yes.' He paused. 'I did not know you knew the German language. Does Miss Malherbe?'

'You will have to ask her yourself.'

The corner of his mouth twitched slightly as he shuffled papers. The room was nice and clean, cooler than her sweltering cell, with no odour from the toilets. If the questioning continued in this manner of false civility, she could almost look forward to it.

'Miss Schwob, when did you, uh, distribute this poem?'

'I believe it was about a year or so ago.'

'Are you sure of that?'

'Yes.' Oh, I know what he's getting at. He's trying to link us to the Ritz Hotel mutiny. When was that? I think in May of last year; I remember because we remarked on its closeness to May Day. If the poem wasn't out by then, certainly some other letters with even clearer incitements were; thank God he didn't find them. I flattered his English; perhaps he won't try too hard to corroborate my dates.

Lohse shuffled papers again. The nurse brought Lucy a glass of water. She gulped it and remained sitting very straight. Lohse sat forward and took another tack.

'Miss Schwob, do you think the Jews are responsible for the war?'

'No, I do not.'

'Are you a Jewess?'

'You know I am.'

'Do you think Adolf Hitler has improved the condition of Europe?'

'Certainly not.'

'Do you not think that Germany has the right to rule over Europe, given that we are a superior race?'

'I think it's about time you learned to manage with your own territory and stopped invading your neighbours.'

The room fell completely silent; no one wanted to make the slightest gesture that could be interpreted as agreement. The informant's eyes darted around the room. Lucy suppressed a smile. Lohse picked up his papers and tapped them on the desk, lining them up.

'We will talk more soon, Miss Schwob. You will be escorted back to your cell now.'

He nodded to the nurse, who took her by the arm and walked her down the hallway, around the corner, through an increasing gradient of stench, to the cellblocks. She looked at the heavy oak door of Suzanne's cell as they passed it, but could not tell if she was inside or not. They went down the stairs to Lucille's floor, down another corridor to her cell. The nurse tossed two cigarettes and a small box of matches onto her mattress as she led her in, then slipped away, leaving Lucy to inspect them. Lucy decided to reward herself with one cigarette and to save the other for possible barter. She huddled against the far wall of her cell, below the window, lit up, and greedily sucked the smoke in. She blew the smoke on her blouse and skirt in a futile attempt to kill the fleas, carefully saving the ash to use for writing or drawing.

181

CHAPTER 55

St Brelade, Jersey

July 1944

Dawn and hunger woke them. They split a beetroot, guzzled water. Sleep seemed impossible. It rained off and on all morning; they wedged the shed door open a little to catch some breeze. Lying under the canvas afforded some protection in case a stranger glanced through the door or window; they dared to whisper to each other, holding hands dyed pink by the beetroot.

Peter told her a little about his journeys of horror in the Channel, first to Alderney, then to Jersey. He could not yet mention Juan. She told him about her escape to St Brelade, about Lucille and Suzanne, about her fears for them in prison. He told her about Pauline and Dieter; her hand, her whole body suddenly stiffened.

'What did Pauline look like?' she asked in a tight voice.

'She was tall.'

'Did she have red hair?'

'Yes. Why?'

'Oh, no. Oh, no.' She turned away from him; he could feel her shaking. 'Marlene. What is trouble? What?'

'Was – was she all right? Did she go to prison?'

'I don't know. We all ran in different places when the Germans came.'

'No, I mean had she been in prison before you met her?'

'Yes. I think that is how she hurt her leg.'

'Oh, God! I did it to her! I betrayed her!'

182

'What is this, Marlene? What you mean?'

Between sobs, she was able to slowly tell him.

'A long time ago, I saw her with a German. I thought she was a jerrybag. I thought she informed on me. When I saw her again on the street when I was with Lucille and Suzanne, I told them she was a jerrybag. They knew who to tell. I did that to her, and she was really a heroine! I could have killed her! Oh, God, I was so stupid! It's my fault, whatever is wrong with her leg! Whatever they did to her!'

He was desperate to quiet her; her crying was so loud.

'Marlene,' he said, his panic rising, 'please do not cry. Marlene, you did not know. She was all right. She was very smart woman. She had job at the hotel and she stole food for us all the time, and never get caught. She helped the poor soldier, Dieter, and the Jewish lady.'

She struggled to control herself. She finally managed to croak out the words, 'What Jewish lady? I knew all of them.'

'Miss Viner, a teacher.'

She sat up; he tried to make her lie down again but her face was wild, flushed.

'Viner? Viner?'

'Yes, an older lady. She was very nice. She teach me English. I hope she escape all right. I hope she in someone's house.'

'I destroyed her identity card. Oh, God, this is crazy! Am I a good person or a bad person?'

'You a very good person, dear Marlene.'

'No, NO! I don't know!'

She spent the rest of the muggy day passing in and out of sleep, her head pounding as if blacksmiths were inside her skull. Occasionally she got up, went outside as far as she could go before she was overtaken by violent vomiting. Peter, distraught, tried to let her sleep. As soon as darkness came he slipped out and looked for food.

She was sleeping in the dark when he returned.

'Marlene, please eat. I have some rabbit and a bottle of milk. It is very good.'

She sat up. She felt empty of everything. She took the meat and milk and ate and drank slowly, not saying anything to Peter as he ate quietly in the dark.

CHAPTER 56

St Brelade, Jersey

July 1944

Every evening Marlene would wake up and the problem would be sitting on her chest: was she good or bad? Peter felt helpless. On days when she was able to convince herself that she was good, she helped Peter find food, washed rags in the stream, held him when it wasn't too hot during the day. On days when she was convinced of her carelessness and evil, she stayed under her pile of rags, ate nothing, drank a little water, and rehearsed conversations with Pauline. I didn't know, I was afraid for my life, I'm a bad person, I'm responsible for your lameness, you can punish me in any way you wish.

Pauline would never answer with kindness or forgiveness on the evil days. Do you know what they did to me? Do you know what it did to my mother? Do you know how many people died because of you?

Peter did not understand this daily court she convened for herself. His English wasn't good enough to enable him to discuss this with Marlene much, except to testify, 'You are good, Marlene. You always do what you think right.' He was far too much in love with her now to consider this behaviour to be a liability.

CHAPTER 57

Gloucester Street Prison

August 1944

Second Interrogation

Lucy was let out by Otto, and escorted down the hallway and up the stairs by the nurse. She sat up straight in the proffered chair and observed the same cast of characters. *Major* Lohse looked the same, shuffling papers while looking out into space, thinking of God knows what. Everyone else wore serious expressions probably practised for this situation. After a few minutes, Lohse looked up at her.

'Miss Schwob.'

'Yes.'

'Today I want to ask you about a document labelled as a "Song", which mentions the various fronts of the war, implies the soldiers' wives are bearing children by other men, and, most serious of all, urges the troops to "overthrow our masters". Are you familiar with it?'

'Yes.'

It was rather pathetic, the way he dragged the items out, trying to make a tidy case.

'This, too, is signed by the "Soldier Without a Name". Did you have anything to do with it?'

'Yes.'

'It is very serious, Miss Schwob, to incite mutiny. Are you aware of that?'

'Yes, I am. It is also a very serious thing to invade another country for no reason.'

Lohse looked pained, as if he had just bitten his tongue.

'We shall not discuss that, Miss Schwob.'

'Very well.' Her flea bites were itchy, but she tried not to scratch in front of her inquisitors. She inhaled deeply, savouring the clean smell of the room.

'But you do admit writing this "Song"?'

'Yes, I do.'

He looked at it again, frowning. 'It is vulgar,' he said, not looking up at Lucy. Then, as if he were a powerful critic trying not to crush young talent, he continued, 'But there are types of men on whom this kind of thing would be very effective.'

Does he want me to thank him? Lucy wondered, amused. The session ended abruptly. Instead of being returned directly to her cell, Otto locked her in the tiny courtyard where she sometimes exercised. It reminded her of ballet scenery by Utrillo, a tall expanse of masonry, slightly claustrophobic. She had a little energy today, grabbed a horizontal iron bar and swung from it, stretching her arms deliciously. She could hear many of the other prisoners, shouting to the jailers, talking to their cellmates. A few waved to her from their grimy windows. She imagined herself a ballerina in costume, playing some female ascetic, and stretched her bony frame with the help of the bars. Then Otto returned, and took her back to her cell.

CHAPTER 58

West Winds,
Portelet Rd,
St. Brelade's

Sept. 17th, 1944

[To:] The Bailiff

Dear Sir,

I am just stating the following facts re my wrongful evacuation to France and Germany from Feb. 13th. 1943 to April 25th. 1944. I wish to put in a claim through the British Government on the following grounds, the facts concerning myself as stated at the Aliens' Office were not explained at College House I was already in France by that time it was too late I had to go on to Germany to open my case as I was catholic on my mother's side I would on no account have been taken away I have the letter fm Col. Knackfuss granting my return on these grounds but there was a lot of delay as all the papers etc had to go to Berlin via Stuttgart and Paris. I went alone and left my two small children here and my husband who was ill most of the winter and is still far from well today also my boy was fretting and under the doctor's care most of the time I was away. My home and everything has all been neglected also I have lost all my personal stuff it is somewhere on the continent I shall never see it again I value it at the very least £50 and £5.16.0 I have had to pay out for necessary winter underwear which is very hard considering my husband's business has been closed since last January by order of the German Authorities. I wish those facts stated to the representative of the British Government who is dealing with such cases I can give all the necessary details and letters at a personal interview.

I went to register at the Aliens Office at the time an order was brought out concerning Jews as I am of Jewish origin on my Grand-father's side only I thought at the time it concerned me but if all the facts concerning myself had been fully explained to the German Authorities, there would have been no question of my being sent away I wish to know why these facts have been suppressed and wish the matter gone into, on these grounds I claim compensation and also for the loss of my clothing etc and expenses I have had to meet since coming back which would not have occurred otherwise.

Thanking you,
Yours Faithfully,

(Mrs) P. Lloyd.

==

23rd September, 1944

The Bailiff of Jersey.

Sir,

With reference to the attached letter which you received from Mrs Lloyd, of West Winds, Portelet Road, St. Brelade, I have the honour to report to you that Mrs Lloyd registered at this office under the Order concerning the registration of Jews in Jersey (Registered by Act of the Royal Court, dated October 21st. 1940). A copy of the completed registration form, signed by Mrs Lloyd,

189

is forwarded to you herewith, in duplicate, for your information.

In each case of registration, the person concerned was told by me that the responsibility for registering or not registering under the Order rested entirely with the individual concerned, and Mrs Lloyd was informed accordingly.

I wish to state, in conclusion, that I had no knowledge whatever of the intended transportation of Mrs Lloyd and other registered Jewish persons in 1943 until after it had actually taken place.

I have the honour to be, Sir,
Your obedient servant,

[Clifford Orange]
Chief Aliens Officer.

CHAPTER 59

St Brelade, Jersey

31 October 1944

They were eating a raw swede with sour milk when the frenetic staccato of anti-aircraft fire startled them. They stood, holding the crude double sleeping bag Marlene had cobbled together around themselves, and looked out the little window. The night sky was malignant with tracer bullets and live fire. Suddenly, a plane seemed to stagger downwards; unlike most flyovers, it was fully lit up.

'Those lights mean they surrender,' whispered Peter. 'They should stop shooting.'

Marlene held her breath. The shooting continued, and the plane shuddered out of sight, in the direction of the bay. They could not see what was illuminated in the searchlights: soldiers crowding around the plane in the shallow water, pulling out dead crew, unable to look at the pilot wading to shore, shaking his fists and cursing them, shaming the two officers who finally took him into custody.

Marlene began to cry. Peter held her close in the frigid darkness, began to murmur something, by turns guttural and sibilant.

'What are you saying?' she asked.

'A prayer. I do not know why. I do not believe in a God.'

'What is the prayer?'

'*Yisgadal v'yiskadash shemey rabah.*'

'What is that?'

'It is a prayer for the dead.'

'Is that Polish?'

He chuckled. 'No, it is Hebrew, or something like Hebrew.'

'I had forgotten you were Jewish.'

'So had I,' he said.

She did not quite understand what he meant, but, sensing his discomfort, did not pursue it. She felt for her coat, dug around in the now-ratty lining, and found the cup.

'This was my father's,' she said. He felt it with his fingers.

'Oh, this is *kiddush* cup. You father, he was Jew?'

'Yes.'

He felt he might as well tell her a little about the Spanish Civil War.

'There were many Jews in the Dombrowskis.'

'Who were the Dombrowskis?'

'We were International Brigade in Spanish war. We fought against Franco, against fascists, but we lost. We retreat and the French put us in camps. I was in Le Vernet camp before I go to Alderney.'

'Why didn't you go back to Poland?'

He sighed. 'I cannot go back to Poland. Nobody from Spanish war can go back to Poland. They signed papers in Munich in 1938 to make peace with Nazis. We cannot go back. We are not citizens any more. Do you remember the Munich meeting in 1938? Was it on wireless?'

'I don't remember. I did not pay attention to those things.'

'Ah, *maidel*, many people did not pay attention.'

'So you went from one war to the next.'

'Yes, but I was not prisoner in Spanish war. Now I am prisoner of Nazis. But Pauline' – as soon as he said the name he wanted to take it back – 'and now you, my little *camarada*, my little *maidel*, saved me.'

'I didn't save you, Peter, I just escaped to your hiding place. I … I am not even a help to you.'

'Yes, you are, *camarada*. You are help.'

'Finish your prayer.'

He finished. She said 'Amen' with him. Then, to be helpful, she fiddled with the crystal set and found him music.

CHAPTER 60

Gloucester Street Prison

October 1944

Tapping on her pipes interrupted her thoughts after the latest interrogation. The Germans were going through the motions of preparing to hold a trial. Micky, a captured Jersey escapee in the basement, was signalling her. She bent to the ground and whispered through the hole.

'Hi, Micky. I'm back. Want a cigarette?'

'Yes, please, if you can spare it.'

She dropped the cigarette down the opening, sending it on its way through ancient dust and mouse shit to its recipient.

'What's up tonight?' she whispered.

'I'll pass you some news. I think we'll also have a concert.'

'Wonderful!'

That night, after their 'dinner', Micky and his cellmates, at Lucy's request, sang some old Jersian songs for her, accompanied on an ancient harmonica and much enthusiastic beating on the pipes. The guards did nothing. News was whispered up to her; someone had a radio, or a relative with a radio who visited. 'Rommel committed suicide! The Allies besieged Aachen and bombed the hell out of it! Thousands of jerries surrendered! Maybe now they'll call it "Aix-La-Chapelle" again!'

All they needed was some food; unfortunately, things were as bad on the outside as they were inside. Edna, one of their St Brelade neighbours, was able to bring them the occasional half-loaf of bread or beetroot syrup or apple, but she couldn't manage the bicycle ride over very often. It was difficult enough managing to live on the outside, spending hours scrounging for bits of firewood, trying to make something edible out of potatoes and shrivelled swedes.

The next morning, after a relatively uninterrupted night's sleep, Lucy winked at other prisoners at the bath as they filled their basins. Otto seemed to allow her to interact with others, as long as she did not see Suzanne. She lugged her heavy basin back to her cell and was locked in by a jailer. As she was rubbing the cold water into her face, Lucy heard Otto's heavy step coming down the hall, along with another man, who turned out to be Lohse, looking preoccupied as usual.

Lohse stopped in front of her cell and called to Otto, 'The little one comes, too.'

Otto looked outraged; he expended so much effort keeping Lucy and Suzanne separated.

Lucy's heart pounded as he unlocked her cell door and let her out. It continued its thumping as she was escorted down the corridor and up the stairs to the hearing room, where Suzanne sat in front of the nurse. Their eyes locked as she sat next to Suzanne and Lohse took his place beside the Unknown Soldier. Suzanne looked thinner, of course, but very strong. She gave Lucy a fleeting smile; more would be frowned upon by the Krauts. Lucy's heart swelled with love. She managed to touch Suzanne's arm as she sat down; this was overlooked.

Oberleutnant Lung and *Oberst* Sarmsen strode into the room and saluted Lohse. Lohse turned to the women.

'This is *Leutnant* Lung, who will prosecute at your trial.'

They nodded at him. He looked at them the way one might look at naughty dogs who had soiled the floor. Sarmsen did not look at them.

Lucy looked at Lohse and asked, 'And when does our trial begin?'

'In a week or two.'

'Do we have a defence counsel?'

Lung looked more disgusted. 'Yes, Miss Schwob, you will have *Oberst* Sarmsen.'

Wonderful, they both thought. One of the men who arrested us. The *Oberst* then turned to them. 'May we discuss your case now?'

Lucy had to fight not to give a flippant answer; Suzanne was perfectly composed. This difference in dealing with enemies would be one of the few bones of contention between them.

'Yes,' Lucy managed to rasp, 'let us discuss it.'

They were left alone with Sarmsen, who began to explain.

'In the New *Reich*, the role of the Defence is not, as in other countries, to pretend against all truth that the guilty are innocent. It is limited to stressing extenuating circumstances and pleading in mitigation.'

'That is very reasonable,' replied Lucy. Suzanne looked at her apprehensively. 'But in our case it does not apply. The Defence could hardly deny facts that we have admitted from the very moment of our arrest.'

'But you were also in possession of a wireless, which broadcast misleading and bestial propaganda from the enemy, which influenced you negatively, causing you to commit serious crimes. That is mitigating, Miss Schwob.'

'I take it,' Lucy said, managing a polite tone that momentarily reassured Suzanne, 'whatever the charges are in the administration of justice in the New *Reich*, Counsel for the Defence is not expected to insult his clients?'

Sarmsen paused again, clasping his hands together. 'But your Counsel has not insulted you.'

'I suppose that insult must always be a matter of personal

feeling. Still, if anyone told you that you had allowed yourself to be influenced by a propaganda which appealed to the lowest instincts of human beings, I think you would not like it.'

She coolly observed his reaction, one of clasping his hands even more tightly together, the knuckles turning white. 'If you were conducting your own case, what would you say?'

Well, now he'll know I'm getting some outside information. So be it, she thought. She took a deep breath, cleared her throat, and looked at him.

'I think that I would have asked you one question: If, at this very moment, you were told that, in Aachen, two German women were doing exactly what we have done here, would you blame them?'

He sat up straighter; his hands clasped even more tightly, shaking. If this were not a matter of life and death, if he did not represent the evil of the fascist state, she would have felt sorry for him.

'What do you mean by "Aachen"?' he asked, licking his dry lips.

She phrased carefully. 'It is known that Aachen has been bombed severely, and is under siege. Would you blame German women if they spread propaganda to the Allies, urging them to desert?'

'But, Miss Schwob, that is a different case entirely.'

'Is it?' He now looked impatient. She could not see Suzanne's face.

'Miss Schwob, we are not besieging and bombing you.'

'You are starving us, deporting us and arresting us.'

'Those are people who work against the *Reich*, Miss Schwob.'

'I see we are getting nowhere, *Herr Oberst*.'

She did not want to talk to him any more, but she wanted

to prolong her and Suzanne's time together in the room. She turned to look at Suzanne, who at first looked quite grave. Then she pressed the corners of her mouth together in something Lucy thought was a smile. The *Oberst* turned to Suzanne.

'Miss Malherbe, do you have anything to say?'

'No, *Herr Oberst*.' She then broke into a broad smile which, though displaying teeth lost or blackened by malnutrition, was a beam of pure light to Lucille.

The *Oberst* said nothing for a moment. Then he rose and called for a guard. He did not look at Lucille or Suzanne and remained standing as a young *Feldgendarme* escorted them into a small anteroom with a table and chairs, decorated with old posters of the Swiss Alps. They were brought *ersatz* coffee in tin mugs by a second *Feldgendarme*. Soon, as if they were in a café on Bath Street, they were chatting in English, French and German about Switzerland. After about fifteen minutes of feeling like normal human beings, they were startled by the door opening. The *Feldgendarmen* sprung to their feet as Sarmsen appeared in the doorway.

'I do not think we will discuss this further today,' he said with a note of relief in his voice. 'The *Major* is scheduling your trial for mid-November. Please think about what we talked about before coming to our next meeting.'

The women nodded. Sarmsen left, and the *Feldgendarmen*, acting more like dance partners than prison guards, escorted them back to their cells.

CHAPTER 61

Gloucester Street Prison

November 1944

The guards were growing more lenient, and Lucy was now able to smuggle letters to Suzanne. A rustling and a tube of paper emerging from the opening for the water pipes would be the usual signal for a successfully smuggled missive. She bent to retrieve one in early November, while she waited for the 'trial' that they knew would find them guilty, and possibly condemn them to death.

… a slight Russian advance in Central Europe, according to the names, it must be in Hungary. They say they are managing the Russian attacks in oriental Prussia … but that which is depressing, if it be true, and I'm afraid it might be, is that they say that Churchill would have told the Commons that the war against Germany would not be over before next summer. Did he really say it like that, or did they give his speech the worst interpretation – we won't know. No use in getting sad over it. If they let us live, we will spend the winter here – and undoubtedly, that will be better for us than if they sent us to spend it somewhere else. Let us speak about more uplifting things. I played postman this morning, during my walk in the hallway, Otto being out, the kid from #2 called me and asked me to pass a note on to #7. I protested: but they are Russians! And he said, 'my buddy is with them.' I took the note and went to look through the window of the #7, and indeed saw, besides the Russians, a kid who seemed to me skinny like one of those big

mosquitoes with long legs. Impression accentuated by his position, glued to the wall really like an insect, tied to the open window and looking into the courtyard. I let W. know I had a note for the kid. W. went to pull on his legs while pointing to the door. The kid first thought that W. wanted to let him know a guard was looking at him; he shrugged his shoulders with a defiant look and went back to the window. But since W. was insisting, he decided to get down and come look through the small window. When he saw me waving the note, he broke into a big smile with excited gestures and ran to take the wood off the door, which shows me that he is not the first one [to know that trick]. The third one of the group is downstairs; I didn't see him. The two of our floor are different physically from the common guys we've had in here. More refined. But when they speak in the evening, they have the typical local accent. I had the impression that they were bringing in yet another new person last night, heard coming and going downstairs, and the door of a cell shutting. But I don't know anything specific. Will tell you if I get any info. Vera brought very nice apples; didn't see her, nor E.; when things are such that Otto doesn't let me out, there are no chances. He could have let me go out. It's because Otto wanted to go to the pictures yesterday afternoon when the boss handled some of the outings. But Otto met with a disappointment. When I asked him yesterday evening if the cinema was nice, he answered sadly, 'Nix Kino,' there was no electricity in the afternoon. He stuck me in the back courtyard again this morning. It's becoming a habit. The kid you saw yesterday, if he lives downstairs, must be the one named Claud. The one from #2 was saying last night that they still had two weeks before the judgment. He added the following declaration: 'They can keep me here as long as they bloody well like, they won't get me down.' It's been some time that I've been wanting to send you the words to the song, 'There'll always be an England,' and I keep forgetting. That's what the English deported men sang on the boat the evening they took them away: 'There'll always be an England, and England shall be free. If England means as much to you, as England means to me' I also heard a variant: 'As long as England means to you, What England means to me.' Then there is a refrain with variations on the words: 'Red,' 'White,' and 'Blue.' I find that quatrain particularly moving, compared to common nationalistic songs. They don't ask for glory or crowns, but only the ... right to be that which one wants to be. The other song that is often heard around here dates I believe from the last war. But I was only able to catch some of the lyrics. It goes like this: 'Pack up your troubles in your old kit bag. And smile, smile, SMILE!'

Surely we heard that one before. I was thinking last night, God knows why, about our postman's wife at St. Brelade. Do you remember that on a summer morning, two years ago, we came back up with her from the beach, via Mrs Steele's property. We had just gone to swim and she to fetch some seawater. She told us that the war would be over in 1944, that it was written in Nostradamus' quatrains. He has not even quite two months for his prediction to come to pass. I wonder if she still believes in it with the same faith she had two years ago? Well, you know me, you know how I make use of superstitions. I think of them from time to time, when they are auspicious, because it's comforting, and that one doesn't have many comforting things in this life. But I accept them without believing in them, because if I were to really believe in them, once disappointed in one of them, I would be unable to accept any other, and that would be too bad. Still, I'm disappointed when Churchill's last predictions do not continue, like the last ones, to agree with Nostradamus' – or at least with the postman's

201

wife, for after all, as far as Nostradamus goes, she is the one quoting him. The rain annoyed me last night. It's really necessary, if the Allies win this war, that God be for them, for the weather conditions have almost all the time been against them.

CHAPTER 62

St Helier, Jersey

November 1944

Erica and the latest Russian escapee crouched under blankets in the low-ceilinged cellar. They could hear the footsteps overhead of Germans searching the place; their leisurely arrival gave Erica time to hurry downstairs. This Russian could speak English quite well; they conversed frequently but were silent for this emergency. They both found themselves shifting their positions a great deal; they had little meat left on their bones to cushion them from the hard floor. Albert's clients' farm outputs were closely monitored by the Germans, so it was difficult for them to smuggle out their edible payments to him. Poor man, he had received news of his wife's death in a twenty-five-word Red Cross letter, several months old, from his daughter in Devon. He was so upset, he did not know what to write on the back for the reply; Erica had calmed him down and told him to reassure his daughter that at least one parent was all right. How long would he or anybody be all right? They were starving. But the news they were able to get from the wireless was sounding better. The Germans were at their wits' end; why they were doing this search was anybody's guess. The prisons were full and they couldn't take anyone to France.

Erica had been optimistic that she might be able to end her hiding and return to take care of Edmund, who had grown increasingly frail. This search was a setback, though she had the feeling it was a general search for wirelesses or escapees or any other thing they could find; it would give them the excuse of taking the food in the pantry. Finally the knock they had agreed upon sounded at the door; they pulled themselves up off the floor with difficulty and emerged from the cellar.

'They were looking for a wireless,' said Albert. 'They seemed quite disappointed not to find one.' He chuckled.

Leo, the Russian, scowled. 'They are desperate dogs. Their days will be over.'

'Well,' said Albert, 'they are certainly committing suicide and executing their own at a good clip.'

'So I understand,' said Erica. 'They get shot for stealing food.'

'They think they can steal from the farms to feed themselves, but they underestimate the wiliness of Jersey farmers.' Albert observed, 'My clients are lying low right now, but I think we can count on more sugar beet syrup and rabbit meat soon.'

'One would hope.'

It was still daylight; Albert could not take Erica back to the house yet. As Leo made up his bed in the back room, she asked, 'Albert, when do you think they will have forgotten me? When can I go back to Edmund?'

He looked thoughtful. 'I will miss your company, but I wouldn't dream of keeping you a moment longer than necessary, dear. I think, with all these searches, they still look at their little lists of missing persons. But soon, if the Allies continue with their successes, they will be too busy to notice you. Let's see what we hear on the wireless.'

'Thank you, Albert. Some day, the Dutch government will thank you for what you are doing.'

'Oh, nonsense, dear! It is the least I can do. Look, when it gets dark, perhaps we can play some cards.'

She heard the grief and loneliness in his voice.

'That would be lovely.'

CHAPTER 63

Gloucester Street Prison

16 November 1944

It was hard to feel anything different on the day of the trial. Lucy had written to Suzanne:

> *What I fear is a magnanimous condemnation of 10 to 20 years in prison, and then, when people will shrug their shoulders saying 'it will be only for the duration of the war', that they fly us to Germany to show that the military tribunal's sentences are no joke. Perhaps I see things in a pessimistic way, but to know that their planes are able to go through, even if only 2 a month, brought me down. To be shot here, that's nothing compared to what can be feared to happen over there. Anyway, all we can do is wait, right, and try to keep one's peace of mind – not the easiest thing, my poor little chick. If one became totally sick, maybe that would make matters simpler – but it's not easy either to come up with a real sickness at will. There remains for us courage, focus on stable and dear ideas in order to tune out this painful present, and patience – by having lots of it, it'll have to turn into genius – that famous transmutation of quantity into quality, which always rubbed me the wrong way.*

They sat in the same hearing room, the nurse behind them; Lohse, the interpreter, Lung and Sarmsen all sitting at one table in front of them. Two NCOs were taking notes, trying to make everything look more official. Sarmsen had not been able to mount much of a defence; Lucy and Suzanne had admitted

205

to everything. He looked despondent in spite of his effort to appear indifferent; looking indifferent was Lohse's specialty.

At one point a loud explosion was heard outside; they all looked up, saying 'What was that?' without regard for rank. When reassured that it had nothing to do with the prison, they resumed their discussion. Finally, Lohse stood.

'Misses Schwob and Malherbe, please stand.'

They did.

'This *Reich* Court Martial session finds you both guilty of unlawful possession of a wireless set and for spreading hostile propaganda with intent to undermine the German Army.'

They nodded blandly.

'For the wireless possession, your sentence is five years in prison.'

He paused.

'For the propaganda crime, the *Reich* sentences you to death by firing squad.'

Silence dropped upon the room like a net. Then Lucille spoke.

'*Herr Major*, which sentence do we serve first?'

She grinned. One of the NCOs snorted. Suzanne was horrified.

Lohse at first looked enraged, then managed to regain his usual blandness, perhaps thinking that vermin weren't capable of deep feelings, perhaps thinking in his alternate universe that justice had been served.

'This session is concluded,' he barked.

Sarmsen appeared to be trembling. The four officers left. The interpreter turned to Lucy; she and Suzanne had sat down. 'You are not afraid?'

She hesitated.'I am not afraid of the idea of death. Perhaps I shall be afraid when the time comes. I cannot tell.'

'No … no one can tell.'

Lucy was able to quickly kiss Suzanne before they were separated and led out. She was locked in the corridor for a while; the other prisoners, waiting at the windows for news about their sentence, looked crushed as she faced each window and drew a finger across her neck. They answered with clenched fists and then thumbs up. Evelyn, a Jersey woman held in 'preventive' downstairs (for the crime of trying to escape from Jersey), made an extra effort to shuttle notes and treats from visitors' packages to them.

CHAPTER 64

22nd November 1944

The *Platzkommandant*,

Baron von Aufsess informed me on November 20th,
1944, that sentence of death had been pronounced
by the Fortress Court on two women of French
nationality for offences against the Occupying
Authority, which were not offences of violence.

I have since become aware from more than one
source that the knowledge that such a sentence
has been pronounced is causing anxiety and
distress amongst the population, not because of
any particular acquaintance with or sympathy for
the condemned persons, but because of a feeling
of repugnance against the carrying out of a
sentence of death on women.

I confirm, as I told Baron von Aufsess on
November 20th, 1944, that the condemned persons
are not well known in the Island nor is their
position one of any influence.

In view of the great difficulties which are
facing the civil population in the future and of
my desire to avoid anything calculated to arouse
passion, I desire strongly to appeal for mercy on
behalf of the two women in question.

Alexander Coutanche
Bailiff

CHAPTER 65

Gloucester Street Prison

2 December 1944

Suzanne was pacing her cell when keys rattled, the door opened, and she saw their lawyer from pre-war days, Advocate Giffard, enter. She stood still, staring at him. She could not have been more surprised if Charles de Gaulle had just come in for a chat. Otto stood in the background, then proceeded down the corridor to allow them privacy.

She rushed up to Giffard and shook hands with the scrawny, but still dapper, emissary from her previous life. She found cigarettes pressed into her hand.

'*Mademoiselle,*' he began, 'you are bearing up well, I see.'

'Have you seen Lucy?' she demanded.

'No, I have come to see you first.' He made a motion of writing in his palm, saying, 'You wish to convey your wishes to her, I am sure.'

She rushed to her bed, removed some folded toilet paper. He held out a pen and made small talk as she wrote.

'It has been a fairly mild winter thus far. I hope it will stay that way. I enjoy a walk before curfew.'

As he babbled, he removed a folded handkerchief from his breast pocket and held it out to her. Then he dug in his trouser pocket and took out some boiled sweets, still in the wrappers, and a pencil, and some matches. She stopped writing and held the handkerchief open to receive them, nodding her gratitude. She finished the note, slipped it to him and sat down on the bed, motioning him to stand closer.

'Can you help us? I thought this was a court martial, and we could not appeal.'

'Alas, *mademoiselle*, I am not here about an appeal. The *Feldkommandantur* asked the Bailiff to enquire about your property and gave him a caveat. Because you have been sentenced to death, they need to make sure you do not try to sell *La Rocquaise*. The Bailiff ordered me to see you and *Mademoiselle* Schwob, to obtain your assurance that you have no intention to sell your property.'

He looked sheepish. Suzanne stared at him. Then she began to laugh. And laugh. She had to grip the bedframe. The advocate stood stiffly, waiting for her to compose herself.

Finally, out of breath, but with eerie politeness, she said, 'No, *Monsieur* Giffard, we are not making any property deals.'

He looked ashamed. She made no effort to make him feel differently.

'No,' she said, 'it is all right. I know you don't want to spend time in this smelly prison.'

'No, *mademoiselle*, it isn't.'

'Just make sure she gets the note, please,' she whispered, not looking at him.

He called for Otto. He managed to dry his tears before the big German made it down the corridor.

Otto took him down the dark stairway to Lucy's cell.

'*Kleine*,' he called as he unlocked the door, 'I bring you a visitor.'

Lucy was lying down; she did not get up when Giffard entered. The cold and semi-starvation, along with an inability to digest the prison food, forced her to husband her strength. Giffard glanced back at Otto, who was paying no attention and was already leaving the cell, and rushed up to Lucy's side, pressing Suzanne's note into her raw and bony hands.

'*Mademoiselle*, this is from your friend,' he whispered.

Lucy sat up and looked at the folded note, then stuffed it under her shirt. Giffard took another handkerchief from his jacket pocket and gave it to Lucy, who stuffed it, too, into her shirt. Then he fished in another trouser pocket and came up with more cigarettes, matches, pencil, sweets. These were taken greedily and stuffed under the straw mattress.

'Did you just find out we were here?' she asked.

Shame rose in his throat like acid; in a small voice he said, 'No, *mademoiselle*. As I was just telling *Mademoiselle* Malherbe, I am here on a property matter brought up by the Bailiff.'

'Property?' She wasn't laughing.

'I'm sorry. Yes, uh, because of your sentence, the Germans need to make sure that your real property is not up for sale or, as they say, "hypothecated".'

She looked much more openly angry than Suzanne.

'Oh, is that why you came, then? You think I have the deed under my mattress? Could I be smuggling notes out to agents in my slop bucket? No, *monsieur*, it is not "hypothecated", as you put it. It is not.' She rubbed her back, looked at him with irritation. 'So, they want us to die very tidily, then?'

He felt the tears again. 'Oh, *mademoiselle*, I am sorry! I know you are not thinking of such things at this time! I pray for you! It is all so miserable!'

'Come on, Giffard, straighten up! The war could end before they kill us!'

'Yes, it could,' he managed to say. 'I will try to visit you again.'

She refused his hand. 'Thank you.' She looked exhausted just from the short time of sitting up.

He called for Otto, who looked soberly at Lucy as he let Giffard out. Giffard shook hands with a surprised Otto, who found a cigarette and a fifty *Reichsmark* note in his hand.

'Please take care of them,' Giffard whispered.

Otto handed back the note, kept the cigarette. 'I already do, *Herr Advokat*.'

Otto walked slowly back to Lucy's cell and let himself in. This gave her plenty of time to hide Suzanne's note; he wouldn't bother her about the sweets.

'Miss Schwob,' he began.

'Yes, Otto?'

'You are looking ill. You always stay in your bed. I am going to bring the doctor to see you.'

'Are you afraid I will die before I am executed?'

'Please, Miss Schwob.'

'By all means, Otto, fatten me up for slaughter.'

Otto sighed and closed the door softly behind him. Lucy rolled onto her side and rubbed the scabs on her back, the result of skin and bones lying on thin straw. Otto was such a strange mixture of traits, she thought; he adhered fairly strictly to the rules, and was always impassive in demeanour, but displayed great solicitude toward his charges. All in all, the best traits for survival in a fascist state. His superiors considered him to be loyal, and he considered himself to be kind; his conscience was untroubled.

Lucy sat up in bed and took out the piece of paper. There were two drawings on it; one of a baby bird's open beak, a playful sexual symbol they had always shared. The other was of a tortoise with the head and tail of a happy, chubby cat. Both had been drawn quickly and expertly; Suzanne, who could express herself with root vegetables, found paper effortless. There were also some lines: '*My love, I am well. I hope Giffard delivers this, and delivers us. Your little bird-mouth, Suzanne.*'

CHAPTER 66

St Brelade

Winter 1944–45

They had gained a BBC station in Normandy but were losing their food supply. Milk was left out for them, but no bread or swedes. It was getting very risky to try to dig up crops in abandoned fields because the German soldiers were there, doing the same thing, even though it was under penalty of death. They were still moving around at night, foraging, eating, and taking advantage of the warmer daylight hours to sleep.

Marlene had dismissed her inner lower court after it had found her not guilty. Her internal prosecutor was appealing to another court to overturn the verdict. The trial sessions went on most of the days when she could not sleep. Tinkering with the wireless was a better diversion. She had managed to get her hands on a telephone receiver and make another earphone. The broadcasts on the BBC were more encouraging, the ones from Germany more desperately cheerful. She had discovered she had a talent for wiring up the little crystal sets, and was able to build a second one so they could both listen at the same time, even to different stations. It was funny to think that they had the luxury of two sets amid the squalor and starvation of the shed. They had already eaten one rat, roasted during a firefight when nobody would notice the flame. More would probably follow. Peter could differentiate her moods of guilt from her moods of self-confidence and tried to act accordingly. She was able to wake him from his nightmares (he mumbled

213

in Polish and broken Spanish), to hum his favourite music, to love him with an empty belly.

In January, when they were giddy with hunger, food began to appear. A Red Cross ship had finally been permitted entry, bearing sorely needed provisions. They ate tinned peas with stone-hard cheese grated on the ragged lid, mixed powdered milk with water and crumbled biscuits, smelled tea longingly with no way to brew it.

On one of her trial days Peter presented Marlene with a piece of chocolate.

'I don't deserve it,' she said, starting to cry.

'Yes, you do. Please have it, Marlene. You deserve everything.'

He dried her tears, fed her, and kissed her chocolatey mouth.

CHAPTER 67

Gloucester Street Prison

December 1944

The doctor looked like Goebbels, thin and menacing, but had a smooth, low voice. He smelled of coltsfoot cigarettes. He did a perfunctory examination, listening to Lucy's chest, looking at her tongue, taking her pulse.

'I believe you are anaemic, *Fräulein* Schwob,' he pronounced. 'I will give Otto pills for you to take with meals.'

She smiled to herself. What meals? Gruel, a swede, a half cup of skimmed milk? Of course I am anaemic! Do they want me to waste away and spare them the bullet? No, they want me to die officially; that is how they are.

The doctor was ushered out. Otto tossed a half-slice of potato bread onto her bed as he swung the door closed; it looked as though it had come from his pocket. She would not die on his watch! Or maybe he did feel for her, did not want her to suffer beyond what she was ordered to suffer.

The pills made her sick; she vomited most of her meals. The doctor with the scary face and soothing voice was called again; he said that the pills were perhaps too strong for her and gave other pills for her to Otto; she refused to take them, refused most of her food, refused cold drinks, stayed in her bed. He brought her a cup of *ersatz* coffee, steaming if not very fragrant; this, she drank. Otto looked relieved. He began to bring her plates of food reserved for the jailers and officers: bits of potato, cut-up pieces of horsemeat, stewed beans. He looked pained and sad when she refused these delicacies. She grew weaker, told Otto her only desire was for rice and tea.

'Rice and tea? That's impossible!' he wailed, plainly showing his frustration.

He disappeared for a few hours, returning with a small cup of rice and a half-mug of real tea. He fed her like a bird. He began to bring her a quart of hot water every morning, which she would drink plain, or, when the weather got colder, pour from the pan into a milk bottle and wrap with her blanket to make a hot water bottle. She began to regain some strength as Christmas was approaching. Otto or one of the Russian trusties continued to bring her a daily pan of hot water and occasional morsels, which she began to be able to swallow.

Christmas Eve arrived. Evelyn gave Lucy some sweets and bright butterflies made of paper. Suzanne, forever pacing, stopped when she heard tapping on her floor. She went over to the corner where the water pipes came through. A little piece of rolled-up lavatory paper was dancing up and down through the opening. She grabbed it, whispering a 'thanks' to Evelyn below. She unrolled it and smiled to see Lucy's handwriting:

December 23, 1944

I have nothing to offer you for Xmas but a dream I had around 4:00am. It is actually more of a restitution than a gift, for it really looks like a plagiarised version of the dreams you recount to me at times. It has the charm of being totally impersonal. I woke up with the impression that I had just read the page of a book: War causes disorders which are not discussed. Thus, around the equator, where the earth is closer to the sky, the

friction caused by this excessive agitation caused a great num-
ber of stars to become undone. These can be found dead or
dying along the railways. From looking at the sky, there are so
many left that it can't be noticed, and men hope that God will
not notice. But it's nonetheless wise to clean up any traces of
this accident. So they dug two big pits, and, just like a dishon-
est servant puts in the ground broken dishes, they buried the
dead stars. And so that their children forget what they contain,
they gave those tombs incomprehensible names. The one which
is to the south of the equator is called, 'The Voice of the
Elements' and the one to the north, 'The Virgin's Mouth.'

Merry Xmas 'Anyway'!

Evelyn tapped again and passed her a thin paper parcel of
sweets, cigarettes, and butterflies.

That evening, after a trip to the lavatory, Suzanne's jailer,
one of the trusties, forgot to lock her cell door. She waited until
midnight to enjoy her freedom. She slipped out of her cell and
walked down the hallway. A man sat on the steps; she had not
seen him before. He was an American pilot, a Lieutenant Haas.
His cell, too, had been left unlocked, perhaps due to holiday-sea-
son laxness, perhaps on purpose. He had been given the best cell,
the one reserved for German officers. He was young, open.

'Don't worry, *Mademoiselle* Malherbe,' he boasted, 'I'll get a
message to my colonel here before we break out. He won't let
anything happen to you. He'll get back at – '

'Quiet,' Suzanne urged. 'You shouldn't let on what you
think or plan, or anything. They will find out. You should just
be good and quiet and make your plans secretly.'

'Yes, ma'am. That is good advice. Anyway,' he lowered his

voice further, 'I want to collect information from prisoners to use against the Krauts when they surrender.'

'Please, God, let it be soon!'

'Yes, ma'am! I think it will be. Things are not going well for them in the Ardennes.'

'Excellent! I can get you something.'

They chatted awhile, then Suzanne went downstairs to Lucy's cell, feeling her way in the darkness. She rapped softly on her door.

'*Cherie*,' she whispered, 'I have come to visit.'

Lucy was not asleep and jumped off her bed with as much agility as she could muster. She hurried to the door and pressed her fingertips under the door. They were answered with Suzanne's, which were warm.

'Oh, Suzanne, *cherie*, what a Christmas present!'

'Yes, they forgot to close my door.'

'Did you get some sweets and butterflies?'

'Yes! I think we are getting some Christmas parcels tomorrow. Our friend Edna may also bring something, if she has anything. Listen, I met an American officer upstairs who wants to escape.'

'Wonderful!'

'He is very young and sweet. I told him to be cautious. I think he wants to collect testimonies. Shall we send him off with a note?'

'Yes! Can I get it to you tomorrow?'

'Yes.'

'My wolf, my little bird-mouth, I miss you!'

'I miss you terribly. I received your poem. I loved it.' Suzanne fished around in her pocket and came up with a sweet. 'I cannot kiss you, but here is a sweet for your lips.'

'Thank you, my love.'

The cold fingers grasped the sweet, pulled it in, then returned to touch Suzanne's.

'Listen, *cherie*, I am told by this young man that the Germans are having trouble in the Ardennes.'

'That is so good! The problem is that one does not know if they will get more lenient as their time runs out, or more desperate.'

'I think it will be the former, at least for civilians. Have you heard anything about our case?'

'Nothing definite, though I thought I heard Lohse mention Giffard's name the other day.'

'That is encouraging. Maybe the old man isn't the *con* we thought he was.'

'I hope you are right.'

'*Cherie*, I should probably go back now. I don't want to be punished for being out of my cell. Perhaps they will let us see each other tomorrow.'

'Yes, *cherie*, we should not take chances. Goodnight, my love. Courage!'

The cold fingers pressed the warm ones intensely, then withdrew. Suzanne tiptoed upstairs and returned to her cell. In the morning, the jailer said nothing as he turned the key to let her out for a wash and found the door already unlocked. Lucy busied herself with a short note; she put an address in liberated Paris on the back and managed to slip it to Evelyn, who got it to Haas. The rules continued lax for Christmas. Lucy did not meet Haas, but she was able to see Suzanne in the hallway and give her a brief congratulatory hug. Everyone doted on the lieutenant in the cell upstairs, sharing their little Christmas cakes and milk with him, and passing notes to take with him on his inevitable escape.

In early January, on the brink of starvation, with no more butter, sugar or salt available, and only a quarter-pound of meat per month, the Germans finally allowed a Red Cross ship, the *Vega*, in from Lisbon. Its contents were quickly off-loaded. The Germans did not interfere with any of the pack-ages except for the baby clothes, whose English-newspaper wrappings were confiscated (and no doubt read by the confis-cators). All civilians, including the prisoners, each received a parcel with 6 ounces of chocolate, 20 biscuits, 4 ounces of tea (!), 20 ounces of butter (!!), 6 ounces of sugar, 2 ounces of dried milk, a one-pound tin of marmalade, a 14-ounce tin of corned beef, a 13-ounce tin of ham or pork, a 10-ounce tin of salmon, a 5-ounce tin of sardines, an 8-ounce tin of raisins, a 6-ounce tin of prunes, a 4-ounce tin of cheese, a 3-ounce bar of soap, and an ounce of salt and pepper. Everyone in prison made a little cupboard, almost a shrine, out of the box to store these luxuries. A can opener made the rounds of the cells. Often a trusty could be relied upon to heat something up in the little jailers' kitchen. Fortified by the food, Lieutenant Haas made his escape on 8 January.

For Lucille and Suzanne, January lurched on as they waited for their lives to be ended by execution or saved by Allied victory; it was like waiting for the flip of a coin.

The news of the war was getting better; more German retreats. The Germans were getting harder and harder on their own, executing soldiers without trial for the merest intimation of mutiny or other infractions.

Otto did his best to keep all his prisoners healthy, ferrying tidbits and cigarettes back and forth among the squalid cells, still vigilant, however, to any passing of notes.

Suzanne paced and slapped her arms against her body to keep warm; Lucy hugged her little makeshift hot water bottle and sang with the downstairs crew during the long nights. They weren't getting much milk any more; the bounty from the *Vega* kept everyone from starving.

Lucy wrote on toilet paper to Suzanne:

Obscure dreams, crushing and putting back together always
The sovereign waves of our strange slumbers.

January 25, 1945
(six months in the can!!)

CHAPTER 68

Gloucester Street Prison

19 February 1945

Suzanne paced her cell, more conscious of the stone floor under her feet, the dim sounds coming from the outside, the rustle of mice. This might be her last night. They were to appear before the 'court' the next morning. They couldn't just be shot quickly; they had to make a ceremony out of it.

A length of toilet paper was folded close to her heart; Lucy had got it to her that evening.

> *Lullaby*
> *To a woman on death row*
>
> *In a white cell*
> *It's the eternal Sunday*
> *Of which never does a Monday*
> *Interrupt the boredom*
>
> *In the courtyard where I am walking*
> *The old tired wall*
> *Does not even have room to lie down.*
>
> *In the courtyard where I am walking*
> *In the uneventful hallway*
> *Everywhere here, spaces*
> *Are vertical*

Words are strange to us
Like the language of angels.
Friends, what is
The horizon?

These eternal Sundays,
And on the beds made of boards
The unending hell
Of wintry nights.

O fourteen-hour long nights
Where dreams are
Our only recourse
Velvet nights.

It is freezing weather.
A cat the colour of ash
Upon my heart melts
Lies down in a circle.

Voice the colour of smoke
Which in the appeased night
Softly calls out:
I am waiting for you.
The sun upon the sand …
Barely believable.
Gardens are too green.
So that's the sea?

Tomorrow maybe at dawn.

Despite the lullaby, she couldn't sleep. She was almost relieved when they came for her. First a trusty handed her a
container of water so she could wash before appearing before
the court. She quickly availed herself of it. Then the nurse and
interpreter, along with a grave and sleepy Otto, escorted her to

223

the room where she had undergone so much questioning, where she had last been able to see Lucille clearly.

She sat down; Lucy was not there yet. An unfamiliar officer sat in front along with the two NCOs she had seen before. He looked as if he had been up for a while and had just breakfasted on coffee and sweet rolls. His uniform fitted him perfectly; he was freshly shaven. He avoided her eyes.

Lucy was then led in, looking serious but not as ill as she had looked before. Suzanne locked eyes with her for as long as she could. Then Lohse and Sarmsen came in. Lohse was looking, she thought, a little sheepish. They saluted the new officer, whose name was Koppelmann, and the non-coms, and sat next to Koppelmann. There was rustling of papers and clearing of throats. Suzanne started to tremble.

Koppelmann spoke up. 'You are Miss Schwob?' he asked Suzanne.

'No, I am Miss Malherbe.'

He turned, expressionless, to Lucy. 'You are Miss Schwob?'
'Yes.'

'This session of the court martial is called to order. The court has reviewed your sentences.'

They looked straight ahead, expecting formalities followed by death.

'The court has decided to commute your death sentences to life imprisonment. We have received communications from Bailiff Coutanche and from your attorney, Advocate Giffard, advising us that it would be … ah … inconvenient for the *Reich* to execute two women on the Island of Jersey.'

Suzanne smiled. Lucy sat expressionless. Sarmsen looked at them coldly. Maybe this was not good for his legal career. Their civilian lawyer and the Bailiff had succeeded where he had not.

'In one sense you will still be in solitary confinement, but you may now share a cell.'

This finally brought a smile to Lucy's face.

'Does Defence Counsel have anything to say?'

'No, *Herr Major*.'

'This *Reich* Court Martial is dismissed.'

The officers rose, gave their Hitler salutes, and filed out.

Otto came in as the officers were leaving; he saluted them, not too smartly. Lucy and Suzanne, numbed by the news, suddenly brightened when they saw Otto, giving him little hugs; then, seeing he had no objection, shared their first kiss since November.

'Misses Schwob and Malherbe,' he began –

'Yes, Otto?'

'Which cell do you wish to share? Tomorrow we will put you together.'

That was easy. Lucy's cell, number five, was larger and better-ventilated. They said in unison, 'We would like number five.'

'*Jawohl. Große*, uh, would you prepare any belongings you would wish to take?'

'Yes, Otto.'

They were escorted by Otto and the nurse back to their cells.

CHAPTER 69

St Helier, Jersey

4 March 1945

It was cold but sunny. Erica, her hair dyed black, shielded by dark glasses, sat in the back garden, away from prying eyes. The sunlight was almost as good as food, warming her face. She had borrowed a book from Albert's little collection, but kept turning her face to the sun and closing her eyes instead of reading it. A few people came and went on the quiet road outside; she was protected by a tall wooden gate.

Her reverie was broken by the sound of two men speaking German. She was startled, but their talk did not sound of an official nature. Rashly, she stood and walked over to the gate to peer between the boards. Two young soldiers were walking with a bundle between them; as they got closer, she saw that it was a tennis net. Wrapped inside of it were several large fish. An interesting use for a tennis net, she mused. I wonder who won the set?

She let herself back into the house and told Albert about it; he laughed, really laughed, for the first time in a while.

'I might have a tennis net somewhere,' he said. 'I wonder if they want to fish doubles?'

A few days later, explosions rocked the town; the Palace Hotel had caught fire; this in turn set fire to an ammunition dump. A shed in a nearby *Todt* depot also burned. It was widely rumoured to be the result of sabotage by the German Marines, who had been running wild, stealing potato bread from the bakeries, daubing houses with swastikas. The

Feldpolizei were afraid to take them on. Erica took this flourishing of anarchy to be a very good sign.

It was another very good sign when the *Vega* docked with a huge cargo of flour. Real loaves of bread soon appeared in the bakeries, enough for everybody. Erica, Leo and Albert sat at the little table in her bedroom and ate bread and butter, tears streaming down their faces.

'Erica,' said Albert, 'I think soon it will be safe for you to go home.'

She beamed; Leo patted her on the back.

'I will go and see Edmund today or tomorrow,' Albert went on, 'see how he is doing, and see how the neighbourhood looks. I think that if there is another big sabotage act, or some other distraction, like a mass German suicide, ha ha, you might be able to walk down the street without being noticed.'

'Oh, I hope they start the mass suicide soon! It makes me want to play funeral music out the window to encourage them!' she said.

'They are doing a good job themselves without encouragement,' observed Albert.

'No, we must hurry them!' shouted Leo after swallowing a mouthful of bread. 'Albert, do you have such music?'

'Yes, but I cannot play the gramophone without electricity, Leo. Also, it will call attention to me. What is really wonderful for us and bad for them is the wearing of the red-white-and-blue rosettes, sometimes on the right side of the lapel, that I have noticed. The Germans aren't doing anything about it.'

'The British colours? Oh, that is good!'

The next day, more explosions. The Germans were demolishing the ruins of the Palace Hotel. Albert knocked on Erica's door.

'Shall we go for a stroll, Erica? They are demolishing the hotel.'

227

'Yes!'

She was ready in an instant; she put on her dark glasses and smoothed her dark hair, grabbed an embroidered pillowcase. They set out, looking like an average couple out to queue up for food, paying no mind to the frequent booms coming from the Palace site.

They made their way to Dicq Road. She still had her keys. They knocked so as not to startle Edmund, and then entered. The house was much darker than she remembered; it smelled of boiled cabbage. She tiptoed over to Edmund's bed and paled; Albert had not prepared her for how he looked, shrunken and fragile.

'Edmund,' she whispered hoarsely. His eyelids fluttered open and she was relieved to see the same twinkle, like diamonds in a skull. 'Ohhhh,' he sighed. 'Is that my little Dutch girl? What happened to your hair?'

She grabbed his hand and kissed him, her tears wetting his face. Albert turned towards the door.

'Wait, Albert!' she cried, turning back to Edmund. 'Edmund, he saved my life!'

'I know, dear. Albert, my man, I've said it before, you are a prince among men! Thank you for saving Erica and bringing her back to me.'

'Not at all, Edmund. I'll leave you two now.' He did not want them to see his own tears, and slipped out through the door.

'Do you have rations, darling? We rushed over here, and I couldn't bring much of anything. Oh! I did bring you this!' Erica pulled the pillowcase out of her handbag and began to put it on his pillow. 'I embroidered this for you, Edmund.'

'It's lovely,' he said in his it's-very-nice-dear voice. How she had missed it! 'I don't have much. I haven't been able to get out, dear, and the neighbours have been quite good, but … '

'Do you have ration coupons? I suppose I shall have to go out and redeem them.'

'Yes, look in the cupboard over the sink.'

She looked in the cupboard, which contained a can of peas, a can of salmon, and coupons.

'You have a little food, Edmund. I shall go out and get more.'

Her hands began to shake. She kissed him (would this be the last time?), and put her coat and dark glasses back on, then set out.

She hadn't noticed much on her walk over. Now she saw all the trees were gone. People carried railroad ties and odd branches on their backs. Some young boys went by, carrying milk bottles. She noticed two of them had tricolour rosettes on their jackets and felt a little braver. She made her way to the nearest bakery, not the one she used to go to, and looked on the shelves. There was bread! Nothing else, but bread. She looked through the ration book (of course, they could only use rations for one) and handed over the coupon, receiving a loaf in return. She went to the chemist, found aspirin and witch hazel, paid with the money still in her purse from two years before. Nobody paid her any mind. It was wonderful! She was able to find some tea at another grocer's after a terrifying wait in line. She walked back to the house and made tea and little half-sandwiches of salmon. Then she bathed him with cool water and some soap she had found (he had indeed received a Red Cross parcel recently), finishing by rubbing him down with the witch hazel.

'I'll take care of you now, darling,' she whispered to him as he began to doze. 'I think the war is almost over.'

CHAPTER 70

Gloucester Street Prison

Late April 1945

Cell number five could have been more joyful were it not for the increasing frequency of executions. Even Otto was distressed; he would often ask the women for a book or cigarettes for the latest condemned man; they always obliged. But these gifts always had to be at Otto's instigation; when Lucille slipped cigarettes under the door of a recently-executed prisoner's cellmate, Otto saw her. He said nothing to her, but as he was locking all the cells for the night, he began roaring in the hallway, 'They are evil, the lot of them! I get them food, I get them doctors, and still they pass notes and contraband! These undisciplined shits! These fucking ingrates! I cannot stand it! Fuck them all!'

Suzanne interpreted his German for Lucille, who chuckled. 'He is in quite a bad mood, isn't he? I think the *Reich* is done for.'

Evelyn left preventive; they could still wave to her on the civilian side through the hole in the bathroom wall. She was replaced by a near-catatonic, tall young woman who looked vaguely familiar to them. Apparently she was the lover of a deserter who was soon to be executed; she might suffer the same fate. They looked at her limping in the exercise yard, saying nothing, her auburn hair greasy and unkempt. Finally, they realised she was the woman Marlene had pointed out to them in St Helier as the jerrybag who had made trouble for her. This made no sense. They whispered through their channels;

230

this girl was no jerrybag, all the replies said. She was very brave. She had sheltered the deserter and others, and had worked for the Resistance. Several people vouched for her. She had been a tough prisoner until they had brought her lover in and sentenced him to death.

'I suppose Marlene was mistaken,' Lucille muttered, her throat tightening.

'Yes, I think you're right,' responded Suzanne matter-of-factly. 'Marlene was hardly an experienced Resistance member. She cannot be blamed for being a little too suspicious.'

She was a little taken aback when Lucy began to weep quietly. Later, they tried to share their cigarettes with the girl, whose name was indeed Pauline. She mutely accepted one, but was careless about concealing it and a guard took it away from her.

The *Feldgendarmerie* brought in a new prisoner, a Russian. Lucy watched his arrival through a keyhole that afforded a view of a piece of back courtyard. He looked like Gary Cooper. His uniform was torn and blood dripped from his nose, but he carried himself with dignity even as the policemen searched him, tearing his clothes up further and pinning him up against the wall to violate him with a filthy leather-gloved finger. Tears interfered with her view as he was gone over with a truncheon and then dragged away to another building. The next morning, everyone said he had been shot.

Dieter, the deserter, was pitied by the other prisoners but also despised by Germans and Jersians alike for deserting. Occasionally his pale face, proud and wild, was glimpsed in the other exercise yard on the other side of the garden; he would try to talk calmly to Pauline, who could only weep. Soon, he was no longer seen at exercise. The night before his trial, Lucille's sleep was shattered by gasps and moans of pain.

She lay awake next to Suzanne, listening for hours. The next morning one of the Jersian prisoners informed her matter-of-factly that it was 'the German bloke'. Later, one of the trusties, Karlchen, his face tight with rage, said that the jailers were forcing him to swallow nails and knife blades during his interrogations. A loyal son of the Soldier Without a Name! Lucy summoned Otto, gave him tobacco and a can of Red Cross parcel salmon to take to Dieter. Otto returned later, still holding the can. The tobacco had been well-received, but the prisoner was not up to eating … She gave Otto the salmon, unable to look at it.

The trial took place, Dieter barely able to stand. He got the death sentence, as expected. Pauline's death sentence had been commuted. She would be allowed to attend Dieter's funeral after his execution.

The next day, they heard the gunshot. It was an insane race to kill him with a bullet before the peritonitis did him in. Pauline's mother had been in the day before, bearing a grey dress. Pauline had to be helped into it the next morning. She was able to stand unaided during the brief funeral, tears streaming down her cheeks as the guards unenthusiastically sang 'The Song of the Good Comrade'. Then, as the body was lowered, she slid to the ground and rubbed dirt in her hair and on her face. Two guards pulled her up roughly and dragged her back to preventive. She lay motionless on her cell floor for hours; Otto finally let Suzanne in with a little warm water to clean her up.

As Suzanne walked back towards her cell, one of the trusties was splitting half-rotten wood with an axe, shouting in French with each blow, 'This is for Hitler! This one's for Himmler!' A few silent blows, then, 'Another one for Himmler!'

Suzanne regarded Lucille as she was let in and took her place on her bed. Lucille looked more pale and fragile than ever, even though their diet had improved and the weather was intermittently warm. Lucille clenched and unclenched her fists, not looking at Suzanne.

'*Cherie*,' Lucille sighed, 'what did we do? How many corpses has the Soldier Without a Name got on his conscience?'

Suzanne looked at her closely. 'Lucille, I do not, I do not think …'

'No, *cherie*, we had a hand in this.'

'Well, everybody knows this here. They know what the stakes were. They are very loyal to us.'

'Yes, now they are. I imagine when they were being reined in in '41 because of all our leafleting, they hated us.'

'They did not hate us.'

'Well, were we effective or not? Are you trying to tell me we were not very effective, so I feel better?'

'No, ah …'

'I'm sorry. I'm talking about the behaviour of people in normal times. In normal times, you do not do things to get other people in trouble.'

'What? We got plenty of people in trouble in the Thirties! How is this any different now?'

'You are right, Suzanne. I am crazy. We got people in trouble. We had to do it in order to fight the Nazis. We got Pauline in trouble, we made soldiers desert, we were ruthless.'

She was sitting up, resting her hands on her knees.

'*Cherie*, of course in a war like this the decisions are not clear, or rather they clearly can have both positive and negative results. The enemy likes that. They rely on that to keep the population tractable. What am I telling you that you do not already know?'

233

'When you were in Pauline's cell, did you tell her we informed on her?'

'*Mais non*! Of course not! What would it do to her? Are you crazy?'

'We have to make it up to her.'

'Of course we do, but we cannot make everything nice! There are people out there who informed on *us*. Certainly the woman who sold us paper. Do you think she is going to bring us a gift when the war is over? You are making very fine arguments over a very coarse subject! I think you are too emotional over this! There are people out there I want to spit at, to strangle … ' Now Suzanne clenched her fists and twisted up her face in a moment of permitted rage, then took a breath and went on. 'But I have decided it is not worth it for me. I am just polite to them all. That is what you need to do! Look, you were nasty to Giffard, and he ended up helping our case! As for Pauline, we cannot tell Pauline anything. It would kill her. It is narcissistic to think otherwise! *Merde*, Lucy, what would you do? Say, "Pauline, did you start out as a jerrybag and then join the Resistance after your imprisonment, or did we inform on you wrongly?" To hell with your guilt, Lucy! To hell with whether people like us or not! You never cared about that before! All we can do is help her, and help poor Marlene, if we find her.' A tear escaped down her cheek. 'Oh, God, I hope she is still alive!'

Lucille stood up, her heart pounding as much from the effort as from emotion.

'You are my fierce lion!' They embraced. 'You are ruthless and quiet. I am full of hesitancy and guilt.'

'This war is not neat and tidy. History is not neat and tidy.'

'Yes, you are right, my love.'

Lucy nuzzled Suzanne's neck. She felt a tiny easing of the

invisible bands around her chest as Suzanne, calming down, held her close.

The days passed. The boundary between prisoners, at least civilian ones, and guards became more blurred. Everyone was writing or scratching 'any minute now' on all available surfaces. The guards did nothing to stop them. The news smuggled to them from the German radio got better and better.

CHAPTER 71

St Brelade, Jersey

30 April 1945

An exhausted-sounding Lord Haw-Haw gave his farewell broadcast, reminding the British audience that if they had only let Danzig go, the war would not have happened. Marlene imagined him, dressed in a threadbare suit, scrawny, maybe a little drunk, pounding the table with a bony fist as he worked through the various permutations of 'You'll be sorry.' Planes continued to roar overhead, but they hadn't heard any bombing from the French coast for at least a week. In the towns, the most hardbitten Nazis were still nailing up warnings against milk hoarding, but many of the soldiers were hoping for the end soon, overwrought from seeing their comrades executed for stealing potatoes. Hitler was rumoured to be dead, and the Russians were closing in on Berlin. The officers were out of control; when a sailor at the harbour made some statement they did not like, they put him up against a wall and shot him. The weather was crazy; sunshine alternating with rain and hail. Marlene and Peter, nursing tiny flames of optimism, shivered in the shed and nibbled biscuits when they couldn't sleep.

CHAPTER 72

St Brelade, Jersey

8 May 1945

They dozed in the quiet of the early morning, then shouts and explosions awakened them. They hid under their rags until they realised these were shouts of joy and peals of thunder. They sat up and looked at each other, each waiting for the go-ahead from the other to look outside. Rain drummed on the roof and leaked through the usual places. Peter finally stood and looked out of the little window. Marlene busied herself with the crystal set. With the stroke of a pen, the Germans were now prisoners and they were now free. They embraced, shed a few tears, and then pulled on mildewy clothes and stepped out into mottled daylight.

The rain shower was passing. People were making smoky little fires in the fields and roasting hoarded potatoes. Someone was running down the street with a Union Jack. Marlene grabbed Peter's arm, unsteady with surprise. Then she thought, we must go to *La Rocquaise* and see if Lucille and Suzanne are back. She told this to Peter. She laced up her tattered shoes, he wrapped his feet with rags, and they set off for the farm.

How strange to walk around during the day! Cars had appeared on the road, horns honking. Marlene's heart pounded as she and Peter turned the last corner. The house was still standing, though part of the roof was charred. They knocked; no answer. The door was locked. She peered in through a window – things looked messy; doubtless the house had been looted, but it had not been destroyed.

'Peter,' Marlene urged. 'Let's go in. I want to clean the house up for them.'

Peter looked at her. She looked happier than he had ever seen her; of course, he hadn't seen her much in broad daylight.

'Do you think it is OK? Do you know when, uh, they are coming back?' Do you know if they are still alive, he thought, but couldn't bear to mention it.

'Yes, yes! Where else are they going to go?'

It was a good point. They walked around the house until they found a broken window and managed to get in. Marlene's heart sank. The beautiful handmade plates were smashed, the pictures torn off the walls. A fire had burnt up Lucille's bedroom; fortunately, it had not spread. The rest of the place was pretty dry. A few pieces of the furniture remained.

Marlene decided to burn a dilapidated chair in the fireplace. She somehow managed to get it started with some paper. She found a single piece of firewood in the cellar and added it. They actually still had running water; she began heating some in a pot and swept the kitchen floor.

'I am going out,' Peter announced. 'I am going to find food.'

'Be careful,' she said.

'Why?' he asked.

She couldn't answer. He went out. She found some unbroken plates and began to wash them with cold water and the soap residue clinging to the sink. The lights flickered on and off. She began to look more purposefully around the house for food or other useful items. She found a dusty tin of peas under mouldy papers in a cabinet. A thirty-minute search produced a tin opener. She decided to see if there was anything in the garden.

She went out and stepped into the muddy yard. It looked

quite dug up; the Germans, no doubt, had been looting it in the daytime. She saw no radishes or beetroot, but did see the pointed shoots of an onion. She pulled it up; the onion bulb was soft and black but the shoots looked inviting. She found a single potato. She brought these treasures into the kitchen. Soon, Peter knocked on the door, then let himself in. He triumphantly bore a brown-paper package.

'Marlene,' he said, 'someone is giving out Red Cross parcels. Look at this.'

They tore open the wrapping and found tea, another tin of peas, a tin of butter, a tin of corned beef, a packet of cocoa, a bar of soap. Marlene found a dented saucepan and washed it out. Melting butter over the fire, she added the onion greens, then the cut-up potato and corned beef. The aroma was overpowering; they almost could not wait for the rest of the food. She opened the older tin of peas and added it to the pan, relishing the sizzle and steam that resulted. She used the heated water for the cocoa. They stuffed themselves at the hearth. After sponge baths, they sat again to enjoy the embers and fell asleep in their chairs.

A pounding on the door woke her early the next morning; so wonderful to wake up in the morning smelling of soap, hungry but not starving! Peter hadn't heard it and was fast asleep in his chair. She walked hesitantly to the door and opened it. An emaciated Lucille and Suzanne stood there, smiling, with a tall woman with feral eyes held up between them. A handcart stood behind them.

'Oh God,' Marlene cried, and fell into their awkward embrace.

Somehow they managed to get into the house and sit down in or on the sundry pieces of furniture still in one piece.

'Today is Liberation Day!' said Lucille. 'There are British

soldiers everywhere! *Cherie*, do you remember when I said the war would end on a Friday? It is only Wednesday! It is early!'

The tall woman sat in Marlene's chair, grasping the arms tightly. Then Marlene recognised Pauline and turned to Lucille and Suzanne in disbelief. They answered the look on her face by making cautious motions. Lucille took Pauline's hand.

'Pauline, do you remember Marlene, from the office?'

The eyes swung to meet hers. A slow look of recognition came over Pauline's face.

'Yes, I remember Marlene. Hello, Marlene.'

'Hello, Pauline. I … I … '

'*Cherie*, Pauline has had a tragedy. Do not upset her.' Suzanne pulled Marlene aside and whispered, 'She was living with a deserter. They were caught, and he was shot last week. Do not say anything.'

A deserter. Oh, God. The same soldier Marlene had seen her with so long ago? Suzanne saw the little gears of guilt beginning to whirl in Marlene's head.

'Marlene, do not worry. It had very little to do with what we did after you told us she was a jerrybag. Marlene, please … '

Marlene dried her sudden tears and with difficulty returned to the fireside. Pauline was staring into the dead fire, gripping the chair. Peter dozed. He would have quite a surprise when he woke up.

'It is over, it is over,' said Suzanne. She began to stir the ashes, added a piece of wood produced from the handcart. 'We left yesterday. We stayed in town with Violette, that woman who was always trying to convert us to Catholicism. We got some of our furniture back! We got a ride here from some British soldiers. They gave us some tea. I got some biscuits, too. Let's have them.'

'Marlene, who is this man in the chair?' she asked.

'That's Peter. I hid with him after they took you away.'

'Oh, *cherie*, did he help you?'

'Oh, yes, he was very kind.'

'We worried about you so much!'

Lucille had disappeared upstairs. She came back down from the bedroom with a small glass jar. She was laughing.

'My hand cream! It is not broken! My paintings and photos are gone, but I still have my hand cream!'

She opened the jar and held it out to Suzanne, then Marlene. The once-ordinary fragrance was almost too much to bear. Pauline continued to stare straight ahead. Marlene took a dollop of cream, warmed it in her hands, then took one of Pauline's hands, peeling her grip off the chair arm, and began to smooth it into the rough skin. When she started on the other hand, Pauline leaned back in the chair and looked at Marlene.

'Thank you,' she said.

The aroma of tea woke Peter, who stared in momentary disbelief at Pauline.

'Pauline,' he finally managed to murmur, 'I am so happy to see you alive.'

Pauline's head slowly turned to him. She looked at him for a long time, then smiled faintly. 'Peter.'

Lucille broke little pieces of biscuit and fed them to Pauline as if feeding a baby. Everyone else devoured them quickly and gulped the shockingly hot tea.

CHAPTER 73

Both Marlene and Peter had reasons to see Miss Viner. Marlene needed to see someone she knew she had helped, to see if that could adjourn the court inside her. Peter wanted to see the lady who had taught him English as he slowly became human again after the *Lager*. He remembered her brittle mannerisms fondly.

They found her address in an old telephone directory. Her telephone did not work; it had probably been disconnected when she ran away. They set off on bicycles for St Helier. Marlene again found herself taking deep breaths of fresh air to calm herself. Perhaps this meeting would be the balm her soul needed. They rounded the corner to Miss Viner's flat. The building seemed all right, at least from the outside. They made their way up the stairs and knocked on the door. She answered immediately. She looked thin and grey, like everybody else, but also sharp and bird-like.

'Peter! Oh, I'm so surprised to see you! Who is this?' She looked at Marlene quizzically.

'This is Marlene, my friend. She hide with me after we left Pauline's house.'

'Hello, Marlene. Will you come in?'

She looked disappointed that they had arrived empty-handed. She did not offer them anything. Most of the furniture was gone from the dank-smelling flat; they sat on some dusty trunks and a sofa missing part of its stuffing.

'I'm so glad you're all right, Peter,' she began. 'I was worried about you.' She crossed her thin grey legs at the ankles and regarded him wearily.

'Miss Viner, where did you go after Pauline's house?'

She took a deep breath and uncrossed her ankles. 'I found someone else who didn't mind hiding a Jewess in their cellar. It was very cold last winter. I never had anything hot to eat. They made a great deal of noise walking about upstairs. It wasn't nice and quiet like at Pauline's. I didn't have anyone to talk to. The swedes made me ill.'

'But you survived. You were not found out.'

'That's right. Now I have this to come back to.' She limply waved a hand at the bare flat. 'I don't know what to do next. Nobody will help me.'

Peter cleared his throat. 'Miss Viner, Marlene did something for you.'

'What do you mean? I don't know Marlene.'

'Miss Viner, don't you remember me from the Aliens Office? Remember when you came to register?'

'I remember coming to register, but I don't remember you.'

Peter interjected. 'Marlene tore up your registration card.'

'Tore up? What do you mean?'

'She tore up card that said you were Jewish.'

'Oh … What does that mean?'

'They did not know you were Jew.'

'They did not know?'

'No, the card, it was torn up.'

Marlene looked at Miss Viner as Peter explained this. Her face looked puzzled. Then she narrowed her eyes and looked angry, tapping one foot on the floor.

'But you didn't tell me!'

'I couldn't.'

'I thought I had to go into hiding, and now you tell me they did not know I was Jewish!'

Marlene surprised herself by raising her voice. 'I had to

243

escape! They knew *I* was Jewish! I left St Helier the day I destroyed your card. I destroyed mine, too.'

'You didn't tell me!' She stared in silence, then began to tremble. 'You beastly girl! You didn't tell me! What did I do? Oh, no!' She crushed a fist to her mouth. Tears squeezed from her eyes. Peter looked down at the floor. Marlene looked thoughtful as Miss Viner raged on. 'I could have stayed here! I wouldn't have lost everything! Look at my sofa! I had to eat garbage ... '

Peter interrupted. 'Miss Viner, we ate garbage, too. We were in shed. Everybody eat garbage, Miss Viner. Many Jewish people, they were deported. Marlene and Pauline, they were good to you.'

She was oblivious to Peter's protests.

'You pigs, you didn't even bring me any tea! Get out!'

She stood up, the rags hanging off her tiny frame as she hectored them, growing hoarse and breathless. Marlene's heart was pounding. Peter stood, made some clumsy goodbyes, and hustled Marlene out.

'She is tired, and a little crazy,' he said. They walked the bicycles down the narrow street. Peter, bracing for Marlene's tears, was surprised to find her smiling.

'Crazy like me.'

'What?'

'I am a little crazy.'

'No, you are not crazy.'

'No, Peter.' She stopped walking. 'I understand it now. I saved Miss Viner's life, and she hates me. I got Pauline in trouble, and she forgives me.'

'Miss Viner, she does not hate you – '

'No, it's OK. I did the best I could. The war was big, and I am small. I did some good things, and I did some things that I

244

thought were good but were not, but the war did even bigger things, Hitler did bigger things.'

'I do not understand what you say. Why are you talking about Hitler?'

'Peter, I did the best I could! I did the best I could! A lot of it was out of my control, but I blamed myself for it anyway! Peter, I helped people!'

'Of course you did. I told you that always, *camarada*.'

'Yes, but I needed to hear it from someone else. I needed to hear it from Miss Viner, who hates me. I KNOW I did the right thing, to destroy her card! But the war is bigger, and she is crazy, and she hates me, and it is ALL RIGHT!'

Crying and laughing at the same time, she dropped the bike. He hugged her. As he did, she imagined people all over Jersey, all over the world, hugging or sobbing, standing in ashes and thanking God for all that they had or lying face-down and cursing God for all that they had lost, tasting their first cup of hot tea in years, getting the lice out of their hair and clothes, bringing out their wirelesses and little flags, burying their dead or at least saying prayers for them, tearing down blackout curtains, looking up at the sky, smoking real ciga-rettes, getting loudly drunk, looking for a pair of shoes, carefully arranging schoolbooks not already burnt for warmth.

He helped her pick up the battered bike and they made their way back down the coastal road. The weather was warming up. The road was full of townspeople, soldiers, lorries. Some people were standing on the beach; a few were wading up to their ankles in the still-cold water, shrieking with glee.

When they got back to *La Rocquaise*, Marlene took her coat and spread it out on the table. She found a pair of scissors and quickly cut the scattered stitches still holding the lining in place. Suzanne and Lucille were upstairs, trying to salvage some things from Lucille's charred bedroom. Marlene took out the cup, found some money that had migrated up into an underarm seam, found her father's photograph, and pulled her mother's pearls out of the front facing. She looked at the coat, decided not to sew it back up, but rather to use it for new clothes, maybe something for Peter.

Peter looked at the cup. 'It is beautiful. I never saw it in light before.'

'What does it say?'

'*Borei pri hagafen*,' he murmured, drawing on suppressed knowledge.

'What does that mean?'

'It is to thank God, who brings us fruit, fruit from grape-vine.'

She sat down and looked at her father's picture.

'Is that your father?'

'Yes. It was taken shortly before he died.'

'We can get frame.'

A frame. A table with pictures on it. A monogrammed blouse to wear with her mother's pearls. Hot running water. Could she make a life? Could Peter share it with her? Was there a Poland for him to return to, or could he stay in Jersey? Could he teach her how to be Jewish? She had enough questions to go on for days. She turned to look at Peter; he was fiddling with the clasp on the pearls, then stood behind her and fastened them around her neck. She kissed his hands.

'Sit down,' she said. He sat next to her at the table, her dissected coat in front of them like some strange dinner. 'Peter, what do we do now?'

'I do not know, *camarada*. I am just so happy you feel better.'

'I want to be more like you.'

'But you are, Marlene. You are braver than me.'

'No, I mean, I think I want to be a Jew.'

'Ah, *maidel*. I am barely a Jew myself. But there is one funny thing.'

'What is that?'

'I know by Jewish rules, it is through the mother. Your mother, she was not Jew, so ... '

'So you mean I'm not really Jewish? The Nazis said I was!'

'I know, but I think you have to have ceremony.'

Marlene put her head down on the table and laughed. Peter clapped her on the back.

'We will have ceremony for becoming Jew and then we will have wedding. I think you have to have something like fancy bath. I will get my *maidel* a beautiful white towel, and she will marry me in it.'

This caused her to laugh even harder. The others entered the room. Marlene stopped her laughter when she saw Pauline's tears. This was the first of many fragile days; one needed to tiptoe around Pauline, avoid tiring the sickly Lucille, keep Suzanne from worrying too much. Having gone through so much worse, these were joyful tasks.

At night by the fire they all held hands and listened to the wireless with its constant flow of good news. Lucille and Suzanne had found a cat that had somehow escaped being butchered (perhaps it had come on one of the ships) and proceeded to fatten it up. It took to sitting in Pauline's lap, and she petted it hesitantly. Of course, they began to hear of those who were coming back, and those who were not. They had to deal with the bitterness of seeing the Bailiff knighted, the Aliens Officer still at his job. Healing would go on and on; for some it would never finish. History, like a wave, had picked them up and deposited them unceremoniously back on the sand; at least there was some comfort in recovering together.

SURNAME	CHRISTIAN [sic] NAMES	NATIONALITY
BERCU	Hedy	Roumanian. [*Wanted for stealing petrol coupons and giving them to doctors, she disappeared in 1943, some say after faking her own suicide. Hidden by friends and helped by her lover, a German officer, she surfaced after the war and eventually married him and moved to Germany*]
BLAMPIED née VANABBE	Marianne	British (by marriage)(Dutch by birth) [*survived the war in Jersey*]
DAVIDSON	Nathan	Egyptian (by naturalisation) (Roumanian by birth) [*died in St Saviour's Mental Institution, 1944*]
EMMANUEL	Victor	British (by naturalisation)(German by birth) [*used as an interpreter/translator by the Nazis, constantly harassed, he committed suicide in April 1944*]
FINKELSTEIN	John Max	Roumanian [*singled out as a Roumanian Jew, transferred to Tittmoning, then to Buchenwald for two years, then to Theresienstadt, returned to Jersey 1946*]
GOLDMAN	Hyam	British [*retained by the Nazis on Jersey because of his beekeeping skills, he survived the war but committed suicide in 1950*]
HURBAN née BLOD	Margaret	German (formerly Austrian) [*survived the war in Jersey*]

JACOBS	John	British [*slated for deportation, died of TB in 1944. After his death his family discovered he had been skipping doses of his TB medicine to remain ill so they would not be deported*]
LLOYD née SILVER	Esther Pauline	British [*deported to Biberach in 1943, her husband won her release a year later, claiming she was not a Jew. Fortunately, the Nazis did not find her diary, in which she wrote of her intention to go back to ' … the religion that does help'*]
SIMON	Samuel Selig	British [*probably slated for deportation, but died in Jersey in November 1943*]
STILL née MARKS	Ruby Ellen	British [*deported to Biberach; ?returned 1945?*]

ACKNOWLEDGEMENTS

This book would never have come into being without the help of many people. In slightly different form, it was my thesis for a Master's Degree in Jewish Studies from Gratz College. I never would have hatched the idea of a novel had it not been for the comments of my advisor, Professor Joseph Davis, who suggested I go beyond the usual non-fiction thesis. My thesis advisor, Professor Mike Steinlauf, provided much necessary midwifery. I humbly acknowledge all the faculty, full- and part-time, past and present, from Gratz, who helped me learn to tease out the agendas, puns and other delights to be found in Jewish texts. I wish to thank my husband, Thomas Borawski, for all his technical advice and his help in soldering the crystal radios I struggled to put together. I owe a huge debt to the wonderful personnel at the Jersey Heritage Trust, who put up with my varied requests and answered my panicky emails. Béatrice Beer was invaluable as a translator of Claude Cahun/Lucille Schwob's prison notes, poems and letters. I am lucky to have friends, especially Karen Kumin, who are not afraid to give me advice and criticism; I thank them all warmly. I cannot thank Lynne Hatwell enough for believing in the potential of my book and seeing to it that it was noticed. Mary Morris, editor extraordinaire at Duckworth, had faith in my writing and worked tirelessly to see it published; I am eternally grateful to her.

Libby Cone